# MOKOTO THE MERMAN

**Sarah Tavola**

## **Dedicated to:**

Ruby Gwynneth
Lyla Mae
Mia Cinnamon
Ivy Elise
Arlo Caspar
and
Oscar Louie

The incredible people who inspire me with awe and wonder and ensure that life is always sprinkled with a little bit of magic.

# PROLOGUE

Many years ago, long before you were born, a group of fishermen discovered a tiny island sparkling like a jewel in the middle of the ocean. There were no people or animals on this island, just a few, tall palm trees dotted along the shoreline, gently swaying in the warm sea breeze.

The fishermen decided to stop for lunch and moored their old, wooden boat in the crystal clear shallows. It was only when they stepped onto the powdery white beach, however, that they realised they weren't alone.

There, wallowing in the turquoise tide further along the shore, were three beautiful mermaids and a merman. The fishermen couldn't believe their eyes, and neither could the merpeople.

After gazing at each other for a long time in disbelief, the fishermen slowly and gently approached the merpeople and shared their simple lunch with them. Soon after, their looks of shock and fascination melted into friendly smiles and the two groups came to know and like each other.

The fishermen decided to keep their discovery a secret, but they returned to the perfect island as often as they could to spend time with their new, enchanting companions.

Not long afterwards, the merpeople introduced the fishermen to the rest of their pod, who lived peacefully, deep below the ocean waves, in a place called The Coral Kingdom.

Every time the fishermen visited the island, they would bring large baskets of food and drink for the merpeople. They very quickly learned, however, that they loved two things more than anything else: juicy strawberries and black tea.

The merpeople called their generous visitors legpeople and marvelled at how they could walk, run and dance. The legpeople, meanwhile, were entranced by how the merpeople could live under water and leap and dive so effortlessly in their aquatic home.

The legpeople taught the merpeople how to speak English, and the merpeople taught the legpeople how to understand Mermish, as well as some of the basic calls of whales, dolphins and seagulls.

The legpeople soon realised that mermen were quite rare; most merpeople were mermaids, but both mermen and mermaids had very long hair and were impressively strong. They were also very happy and kind by nature. The fishermen admired their friendly smiles, team spirit and laid-back attitude to life.

Over the years, the merpeople noticed that the legpeople's skin was getting wrinkled and their hair and beards were becoming speckled with grey. They moved more slowly than they used to and complained of pain in their knees. Their visits became less and less frequent until one day, the head of the merpeople realised that they might not see their friends again. She decided to present the oldest legperson, a man called Kai Kalani, with the biggest pearl in The Coral Kingdom, which the merpeople removed from the top of the decorated stone arch at the official entrance, as a thank you gift for their treasured friendship.

Soon after, the visits stopped and the merpeople never heard from the legpeople again.

To remember the date of the legpeople's first visit, the merpeople held a celebration every year called The Feast of Kai Kalani. During the feast, the merpeople spoke only in English and exchanged stories of the legpeople and all the wonderful things they could do with their two extra limbs. As the decades rolled by, however, none of them really knew if it was just a mythical tale or if it really happened.

# CHAPTER 1

It was the day before The Feast of Kai Kalani in The Coral Kingdom and all the merpeople were busy making preparations.

The Coral Kingdom was a particularly beautiful area of the sea bed, circled with big, pink conch shells that the more adventurous merpeople had found on their underwater, ocean adventures. Striking displays of yellow, smooth coral burgeoned everywhere, interspersed with stunning arrays of purple topped, gold rice coral.

Close to the entrance and around the vast perimeter, pockets of green and pink branching coral flourished, their blue tipped polyps matching the brilliant blue star fish who lounged peacefully below. Shoals of bright, striped, butterfly fish added moving bursts of colour, while orange angelfish slipped in and out of all the hidden hollows.

During the Feast of Kai Kalani, however, the Kingdom looked especially stunning. The most artistic merpeople were creating murals on shell walls, using only the colours of the shells themselves. These impressive constructions were beginning to take shape and were sparkling in the dappled sunlight, as shoals of merpeople passed by to appreciate the work. Meanwhile, the most acrobatic merpeople were practising their synchronised swimming displays, gliding through the water while jumping, flipping and moving the flukes of their tails in perfect unison, drawing gasps of admiration from everyone around.

Noelani the mermaid was lying on a bed of seagrass and braiding long strands of seaweed to decorate the rock tables. The merpeople loved eating soft, succulent, green seaweed, and during the feast, mountains of it would be consumed, but red and brown seaweed was reserved for decoration.

As she happily hummed away, her mother called out to her, "Noelani! Have you and Mokoto finished the braiding yet?"

"Mokoto's not here. I haven't seen him all morning," Noelani answered dreamily, as she admired her braiding skills.

"That brother of yours! He's never where he's meant to be!"

Mokoto, meanwhile, was too busy having fun to think about the Feast of Kai Kalani.

Out in the watery depths, Mokoto and his best friend, a dolphin called Molailai, were having a competition to see who could race to the surface of the sea first. Molailai's silvery blue body gracefully glided upwards, while Mokoto kept his arms by his side and neatly swished his tail back and forth, with his long, yellow, silky hair streaming out behind him. They seemed to always reach the sun-drenched end at the same time but would have a friendly argument about who was the winner.

Just as they were nose diving back downwards, Noelani had swum over, neatly flipped her tail and glided in their way.

"I thought you were braiding for the feast?" asked Mokoto. "Do you want to come and play with us instead? It would be good to have some proper competition!" He smiled at Molailai, who gently nudged him with his long nose.

"No," answered Noelani softly, "I have to go back. But mother sent me to tell you that if you're not going to help me braid, can you please go and gather more red seaweed, because we've almost run out."

Noelani ran her fingers through her long, orange hair as she spoke, and slowly swayed her orange, gold and green scaled tail so that it caught a shard of speckled sunlight and glistened like a collection of precious gems.

"I'll help you collect seaweed!" Molailai squealed. He spoke in bursts of clicks, whistles and squeaks, a language the merpeople called Dolphish. Luckily, the merpeople understood Dolphish perfectly and the dolphins had, over time, come to understand the strange language that the merpeople spoke.

"See you later then," Noelani hummed gently, as she waved

goodbye and began to smoothly sashay her way back to The Coral Kingdom.

"Come on then!" Mokoto called out to his best friend, "Let's go and gather lots of the red stuff!"

They'd been searching for about five minutes, when they heard a loud, deep call and felt strong vibrations pulsating through the water.

"Nui!" they both screeched as they immediately raced towards their enormous whale friend.

Nui was majestically curving her giant body above and below the water and was hoping to find some friends to play with. When she caught sight of Mokoto and Molailai, her eyes lit up. She was as delighted to see them as they were to see her.

"Will you give us a ride, Nui?" Mokoto asked enthusiastically.

"Of course!" Nui bellowed, "Hop on board!"

Mokoto gripped the dorsal fin on Nui's rubbery, blue-grey back and held on tight as she picked up speed and momentum. He squealed with delight as his body burst into the warm air above, then plunged back into the salty depths below.

"This is the best feeling ever!" Mokoto shrieked, as Molailai swam alongside them, smiling at his friend's happiness.

When Nui slowed down Molailai called out, "Can you throw me into the sky please Nui?"

"Always my pleasure!" Nui boomed back. It was a game they'd played hundreds of times before. Nui dived deep into the ocean while Molailai floated close to the surface above her. Nui then thrust upwards and, as she neared the top, shot a powerful burst of air and water out of her blow hole, which sent Molailai hurtling up into the sky.

When Molailai was as high as he could be, riding the crest of the surge and silhouetted against the bright blue sky, he yelled out, "I'm on top of the world!" Then, as the force subsided, he tumbled back into the shimmering sea, squealing with delight.

"My turn!" Mokoto yelled out eagerly, so Nui repeated the same performance, and blasted Mokoto into the sky, with his long, yellow hair flying everywhere and his brown arms flailing about with glee, flashing the biggest, brightest smile you can imagine. His radiant silver, blue and turquoise tail then thrashed into the water, flipping wildly with joy.

Once was never enough though, so Nui provided Mokoto and Molalai with hours of fun, until the sun fell into the horizon and the evening sky was filled with a beautiful palette of red and orange.

As Nui, Mokoto and Molalai floated in a happy state of tiredness, they all began to hear a faint whistling in the distance and knew that it was Molailai's father calling him back to the pod.

"I'll see you tomorrow!" Molailai clicked to his friends, before he swam off into the brilliant sunset.

"Will you come to The Feast of Kai Kalani?" Mokoto shouted after him.

"Of course!" Molailai answered, as his dolphin sounds faded into the distance, "I wouldn't miss it for the world!"

Mokoto then realised that he hadn't gathered a single strand of red seaweed, so he bid farewell to Nui and hurriedly swam down to the ocean bed to gather as much as he could.

By the time darkness had fallen, like a blanket on the quiet ocean waves, Mokoto had only managed to pick a few strands of seaweed. He was yawning with tiredness, so he decided to head home with his meagre haul and rest his weary head. As he neared The Coral Kingdom, however, he thought he could hear Molailai call out to him in the far distance.

He stopped perfectly still in his tracks and tried to focus on the sound, but it seemed to disappear as quickly as it had appeared, and he began to question whether he had heard it at all in the first place.

Then, just as he started swimming, he heard it again. It appeared to be much further away this time, and Mokoto couldn't quite figure out if it was a porpoise call, Dolphish or something entirely different.

For a brief moment, Mokoto was worried that it sounded

like far-off, frantic whistles, and he wondered if it might be a distress call. The noise soon faded away, though, and Mokoto shook his head gently to try and stop his mind playing tricks on him.

When he finally slipped back into The Coral Kingdom, the merpeople were all asleep. Mokoto was greeted by a resident group of black and white striped banner fish who weaved in and out of his pathway. He passed a spiky sea urchin that had taken up residence beneath a profusion of purple antler coral in his family's garden and brushed his tail against a bunch of orange tube coral. As he entered their peaceful corner of their community, walled by beautiful displays of cowry, calilla and cockle shells, he found his sister snoozing peacefully on a bed of braided seaweed she'd made. His mother was in her own coral enclave, deep in dream world, on a pile of billowing, soft, red seaweed. Her long, dark brown hair pulsated gently with the rhythm of the ocean and Mokoto thought about how content and peaceful she looked.

He gently floated up towards her beautiful face until their noses were almost touching, then shrieked, "Mother! Wake up! Please! I need to talk to you!"

Mokoto's mother sat bolt upright and threw her arms up in shock. Her stunning maroon, gold and silver tail flapped about with frantic confusion.

"Mokoto? What is it? What's wrong? Are you ok?" She cupped his face in her hands and looked into his big, blue eyes.

He stared back at her like an innocent baby and woefully explained how he thought he'd heard Molailai call out to him in distress.

"Oh Mokoto," she gently scolded him, "it's very late and you must be exhausted. I bet you haven't even eaten anything..."

"I have!" Mokoto protested, "Oh no, wait, you're right, I haven't..."

"Well," his mother continued, "your mind does strange things when your body is tired and starving. Molailai will be fine, what harm could possibly have come to him around here? Go and eat some seaweed and get some rest. We have a big day tomorrow."

"Okay," Mokoto meekly agreed, but he wasn't convinced, and as soon as his mother closed her eyes again, he slipped out to investigate the sounds.

He slowly made his way through the calm waters, back towards where he'd been collecting seaweed, trying his best to pick up on any clicks or whistles. He then emerged at the tranquil surface, his face bathed in moonlight, to see if he could sight anything unusual.

Tiny, twinkling stars filled the inky night sky and everything seemed perfectly serene, until a flock of distraught seagulls swooped down towards him. They were all squawking in a frenzied attempt to convey the terrible drama that had just unfolded in front of their eyes. Mokoto tried to calm them down and told them, in his best seagull calls, to speak one at a time.

He extended his hand and the smallest bird quickly fluttered over and landed on it. Through its intense chirping, Mokoto managed to understand the main message: "Molailai's gone. The legpeople. It was the legpeople. A whole group of them. They took Molailai and his family. Molailai called for you but it was too late. The legpeople were strong so they couldn't escape…"

Mokoto gasped and panic gripped his body in a way that he'd never experienced before. His chest felt tight and his hands were trembling.

"Which way did they go?" he muttered breathlessly.

The birds all swarmed southwards, so Mokoto set off at once in the same direction, thrashing his tail as hard as he could to swim as fast as possible.

"Go Mokoto! Bring him back!" the seagulls squawked from above, like an army of supporters, until they changed direction in an attempt to find other sea life to tell them of the news.

Mokoto let the light of the stars and the full moon guide him, and he mustered every last bit of strength in his tired body to keep swimming onwards for hours and hours.

The last thing he remembered was hearing the faint sounds of shrimp clicking, triggerfish chattering and damselfish chirping, so he knew he must be close to a reef. It was this harmonic coral reef orchestra, however, that ultimately lulled him into the sleep that he so badly needed.

His eyes finally closed, like curtains on a nightmarish scene, and his body slowly drifted with the tide.

# CHAPTER 2

It was a beautiful, balmy day in the land of the legpeople and a twelve-year-old girl called Mia was taking an early morning walk along the beach with her mother, Lana.

Mia's mop of long, loose, brown curls bounced up and down as she skipped barefoot along the shoreline, dressed in her favourite pair of well-worn, light denim shorts and a blue, surf club vest top, with a picture of a dolphin on the front, which she was given when she completed her first surfing competition.

It was the school holidays and Mia was chatting to her mother about what she planned to do later, when Lana would be at work. She'd almost lost track of exactly which day it was, though, as the long, happy, hazy days seemed to have melted into each other.

"I'm going to make a shell necklace," Mia announced, as she picked out perfect, little turritella shells from the sand. "I'll do one for you too…and Grandpa!"

"That'd be lovely!" Lana replied, as she bent down to pick up a particularly appealing ormer shell, with its bluish purple, shiny interior gleaming in the sunshine.

The beach glowed the perfect shade of warm yellow in the soft morning light, while the still ocean glimmered in the welcoming sun. There weren't many people around and Lana sighed with contentment when she thought about how much she loved this time of day. She tucked her straight, jaw length, brown hair neatly behind her ears and undid the top button on her formal work shirt as she embraced the heat of the day.

They ambled onwards towards the pier, where the tide seemed to have brought in an unusual amount of seaweed, along with the distinct and familiar beach scents of sulphur and brine.

"Look how much there is!" Mia giggled, as she lifted up slimy handfuls beneath the wooden boards of the pier, letting the jelly-like plants slip through her fingers.

Just when she'd dropped the last strand of seaweed, however, her smiles suddenly turned into a look of shock. Her eyes widened as she focused on an alarming mound on the other side of the covering.

"What's that?" she urgently whispered to her mother, pointing at a pile of straggly, yellow hair next to one of the damp, wooden pillars.

Lana gasped and told Mia to stay exactly where she was. She tiptoed over to what seemed like a mass of seaweed, hair and unusual fish scales, then gently started pulling the seaweed away to get a better look at what was underneath.

By this time, Mia's curiosity had got the better of her and she couldn't resist creeping over too, to see what was being revealed.

It quickly became clear that the top part was a human body, but each strand of seaweed they removed exposed a more astonishing picture. The torso was obviously attached to a long, elegant fish tail, with beautifully patterned scales in hues of shimmering silver, blue and turquoise.

Mia and her mother locked eyes in amazement.

"A merman!" Mia cried out. "It's a real merman! Is he alive?"

Lana rifled through her purse to find her small, cosmetic mirror and held it beneath the merman's nose. Straight away, a fog appeared on the glass. "Yes!" she exclaimed excitedly, "He is! He's alive!"

"What shall we do?" Mia asked, as her elation quickly switched into concern for his welfare.

"We'll take him home," Lana decided immediately. "He's not safe here." She nervously rummaged around in her purse again to find her phone and called her brother, George.

George was a tour guide who took groups of people out on his boat to go whale watching every morning and afternoon. As luck would have it, when he received the call from his sister, he'd just pulled into the harbour, after another successful excursion, and was helping the last satisfied tourist step onto the dock.

As they took turns to shake his hand and thank him, his friendly, green eyes crinkled as he flashed his trademark smile. He was a well-built man with a strong, square jaw, deeply tanned skin and dark brown hair that had been naturally streaked by the sun with thick, golden blonde highlights.

When he heard about what had happened, he ran straight to his pick-up truck and drove around the bay, to the pier, where he found his sister and his niece kneeling next to their remarkable find.

"This is mind blowing!" George cried out excitedly, as he ran his hands over the perfect scales. "It's the most wonderful, unbelievable thing I've ever seen!"

"We need to get him in your truck," Lana insisted, "and take him home straight away, before anyone else sees him."

"Right," George's thoughts turned into organisational mode, "I'll grab him under the arms, you two take the tail."

With a strained grunt, George lifted the merman's upper body off the sand. "He's so heavy!" he exclaimed.

"Of course!" Mia replied, "Look at all those muscles, he must weigh a ton!"

"Careful not to break any of his scales," Lana told Mia, as they gently supported his long tail.

They'd just shuffled out from under the pier, and were making their way towards the car park, when they saw an elderly couple strolling along, hand in hand.

"Hide him!" Lana shrieked, frantically.

"But where?" Mia blurted back.

"Behind there!" George nodded towards the low wall bordering the car park. They stumbled forward and lowered the merman's body as carefully, but urgently, as they could.

By the time the old couple passed them, they were sitting on the wall together, looking relaxed, pretending to admire the sea view.

"It's beautiful isn't it?" the elderly woman stopped to remark to their group. "We're very lucky to live here."

"Yes, we are," Lana responded politely, successfully masking her nervous terror at the thought of them catching a glimpse of the extraordinary, fascinating sea creature lying right behind them.

"We might sit down next to you for a moment, if you don't mind," the old man spoke in quiet, gentle tones, "and take in this gorgeous view..."

"No!" George shouted, far too loudly, before his mouth had time to consult his brain.

The sweet, elderly couple looked taken aback and the man placed his arm protectively on his wife's shoulder.

"I mean, my niece here is recovering from the most terrible bout of flu. I really wouldn't want you to risk catching it!"

Mia then coughed appropriately and tried her best to look sick.

"Oh, oh dear," the elderly woman murmured as the couple took a step back. "Well I do hope you feel a lot better very soon, young lady. The clean sea air can work wonders, you know."

"Thank you," Mia croaked, as the couple continued onwards with their walk.

George, Lana and Mia breathed a heavy sigh of relief.

"Let's get on with it," George insisted, "before anyone else comes along."

They managed to haul the merman through the car park and into the cargo tray of George's pick-up truck without anyone else noticing, then George covered him with some old blankets that were strewn over the back seats.

The roads were virtually empty at this early hour, so it didn't take long for them to arrive at the entrance to Mia and Lana's apartment. Mia went ahead and unlocked the street door, then quickly ran up several flights of stairs to the apartment and immediately started filling the bathtub with water. Meanwhile, George and Lana heaved their exciting discovery up to the fourth floor and were relieved when they could finally set him down in the tub.

Mia's Grandpa Frank, who lived with Lana and Mia, eased himself out of his faded brown, velvet armchair and slowly limped over to the bathroom with his walking stick, to find out what all the commotion was about.

When he saw what was lying in the bathtub, he wheezed and placed his large, wrinkled hand on his chest. "I always hoped I'd live to see this day!" he declared, with a youthful glint in his old, green eyes. "He's magnificent. Truly magnificent! Where'd you find him?"

"Washed up under the pier," answered Lana. "He's either sick or totally exhausted. We have to take good care of him."

"Did anyone see you save him?" Grandpa Frank asked anxiously.

"No," George shook his head with notable relief.

Then they all stood quietly staring for a long while, totally enchanted by the magical creature before them.

Lana was the first to break the silence when she shook herself back into reality with a startled gasp.

"Oh no! I'm going to be late for work. I have to go..." she cried out, and quickly straightened her knee-length skirt.

"Can you go out too please, George?" asked Grandpa Frank, "And buy lots of fresh strawberries and a paddling pool?"

"Strawberries?" asked George with a quizzical look.

"Trust me, he's going to love them."

# CHAPTER 3

Mia and Grandpa Frank spent the rest of the day checking on their sleeping house guest. By evening time, Lana was home from work and George had done the shopping. They'd moved a kitchen chair into the bathroom for Grandpa Frank to sit on and the others were settled on the floor, next to the bathtub.

"What if he doesn't wake up?" asked Mia, as she gazed at his long, white eyelashes.

"Should we take him to a doctor?" added Lana, "Or a vet?"

"No!" insisted Grandpa Frank. "He'll wake in time. We just have to be patient."

Right then, the merman's mouth started twitching, which made them all screech with anticipation. Lana, Mia and George moved closer towards him to study his face for any more signs of waking, when his eyes suddenly opened wide and he instantly let out an almighty scream. This startled Mia so much that she immediately screamed too, so her mother instinctively reached out to put her arms around her.

Once his piercing howl had subsided, he started babbling frantically in the bubbly sounds of Mermish, but quickly realised that he should try communicating in English instead.

"Who are you? Where am I?" he stammered, horrified by the appearance of these odd-looking beings with no tails.

"It's alright. You're safe. We're looking after you," answered Lana reassuringly, while simultaneously hugging Mia and rubbing her own pained ears.

"Where's Molailai?" asked the merman, sadly.

"Who's Molailai?" George replied.

"My friend. He's a dolphin. Legpeople took him. Legpeople

like you. That's why I've come here, to bring him back."

"There's only one place a dolphin will be in this town," nodded Grandpa Frank, knowingly.

"The dolphinarium," Lana added. "There are often rumours about them catching dolphins in the wild and taking them there."

"Don't worry though!" Mia added, when she saw the look of concern on the merman's face, "We'll find him!"

"What's your name?" asked George.

"Mokoto," the merman replied meekly.

"Mokoto the merman! How lovely!" cried Lana. "Well don't you get upset Mokoto, we're going to do everything we can to help you!"

The family then inflated the paddling pool in the living room and set about filling it with buckets of water from the kitchen. They carried Mokoto over to his new resting space and he lay there speechless for a few minutes as he absorbed his unfamiliar surroundings.

Lana and Mia had only moved into the apartment a few weeks before and everything still felt reasonably fresh and new. They'd decided to decorate their new home with a beach theme, so the walls and furniture were mainly white, and the shelves were adorned with sea shells and washed up coral. Bright blue and turquoise scatter cushions, printed with starfish patterns, covered the beige sofa while several large pictures of the ocean graced the walls. Framed photos that Lana had taken of Mia surfing took pride of place above the dining table, and an old black and white photo hung next to Grandpa Frank's armchair, showing him as a young man on a wooden surfboard, skilfully gliding through a huge, barrelling wave. Grandpa Frank often liked to gaze at it to remind him of the bountiful energy he had in his youthful days.

Mokoto struggled to understand how so many images and objects that were familiar to him were here, in this dry, still environment. So Mia tried to comfort him by bringing him a big bowl of strawberries. He took a small bite of one and couldn't quite believe the level of deliciousness. It was as if his taste buds had been supercharged. He put the rest of the strawberry in his mouth, including the leaves, and his eyes rolled with pleasure as he savoured every exquisite burst of its perfect flavour. Unable to control himself, he then went ahead and stuffed six more into his mouth at the same time, relishing the glorious experience, while red juice oozed from his lips.

The family couldn't hold back their laughter.

"How did you know he'd like them?" Mia asked her grandfather.

"That's a long story," he replied with a wink of his eye, "one which I intend to tell you very soon. Now go and make him a cup of black tea, with two teaspoons of sugar, and see how much he loves that too!"

Mia dutifully made a cup of tea and brought it to Mokoto, who'd polished off all the strawberries and was starting to look a lot happier.

Mokoto slurped one mouthful from the mug and gasped with awe and wonder. "How do you legpeople find such delicious things?" he cried out, before drinking the rest of it in one go.

"They're just in the shop!" Mia giggled.

"You must take me there!" Mokoto declared, "So I can gather enough to take back to The Coral Kingdom!"

He spent the rest of the evening answering questions from his inquisitive hosts, describing The Coral Kingdom in detail and telling them all about his family and the ways of the merpeople. They were so captivated and enthralled by the whimsical tales of their charming guest, they lost track of time and only realised how late it was when Mokoto started yawning and began drifting back to sleep.

When George left and Lana turned out the living room light, Mokoto slipped into dreamland and thought he heard Nui the whale's pulsed calls, booming out unhappily in the distance, calling for him and Molailai. The deep, sad sounds floated over the water, across the town and in and out of Mokoto's consciousness, leaving an uncomfortably heavy weight in his heart. While he tried his best to focus on this sombre lullaby of lonely vibrations, he inevitably fell into a deep sleep and escaped his daunting reality for a few hours more.

The next morning, when he woke up, Lana had already left for work. Grandpa Frank was reading the newspaper in his armchair, and Mia was resting against the paddling pool, waiting for Mokoto to stir.

"Good morning," Mokoto smiled when he saw Mia's friendly face, perfectly framed by her soft brown curls. "Please can I have some…."

"Strawberries?" Mia interrupted, as she presented him with a large bowl full of his favourite, juicy treats. "Here's a cup of tea too," she added, passing him an enormous mug full of the prized beverage.

Mokoto was steeped in gratitude and couldn't stop grinning at his new friend.

"We've got a lot to do today," Mia stated, as if she was Mokoto's personal assistant. "First, we have to figure out how we can get you into town without anyone seeing your tail…"

Mokoto's smile faded into a frown as he reflected on how his glorious tail was such a useless burden in the land of the legpeople.

"Then we have to go to the dolphinarium and see if we can find Molalai…"

Mokoto's face lit up again.

"Then, if he's there, we have to make a plan to get him out."

"Great!" Mokoto flashed his pearly, white teeth as he beamed a dazzling smile once more. "Can you also take me to this shop place you talk about please? So I can gather some things?"

"It's too risky," Mia shook her head. "We have to be out and about as little as possible."

"Please?" Mokoto pleaded. "It's just that you have so many useful, wonderful, unusual, pretty things in your home, and you eat such unbelievably delicious food. I want to see where you gather it all from and perhaps gather a few things for myself too."

"We'll see," Mia replied sweetly. "Now hurry up and eat so

we can get started."

There was then a loud knock at the door and a cheerful voice bellowed out, "It's me, your favourite uncle!"

"You're also my only uncle!" Mia told him, as she opened the door and gave George a hug.

"Let's face it though," George grinned, "even if you had a million uncles, I'd still be your favourite, because I'm an all-round awesome kind of guy!"

"It runs in the family!" Grandpa Frank added, peering over his half-moon glasses.

George had just returned from his morning whale watching expedition.

"We saw the strangest thing," he began telling everyone. "There's a lone blue whale a little way beyond the harbour, just hanging around, swimming in small circles and not going anywhere. Even as we got close, it stayed right where it was. It's a giant -probably one of the biggest I've come across -but it has to be the saddest looking whale I've ever seen."

"It's probably experienced some kind of trauma," Grandpa Frank theorised. "Been hit by a boat or attacked by an orca."

"Perhaps," sighed George. "Or maybe its hearing's been damaged by sonar and it's lost its sense of direction. Poor thing."

"No!" Mokoto pulled his torso up straight in the paddling pool. "That's Nui! My Nui! I'm sure I heard her calling to me last night! She'll be waiting for me and Molailai to come back. We're her best friends. My dear Nui!"

Mokoto's face fell as he thought about his treasured buddy languishing near the harbour, desperately hoping for him and Molailai to return. "We have to find Molailai then go to Nui! Before the legpeople capture her too!"

"Well thankfully I don't think the folks at the dolphinarium have a pool big enough for her," George tried to reassure him.

"And we'll get you back to her before you know it," Mia added, sensing Mokoto's spiralling heartache.

"Any ideas how we can get Mokoto into the dolphinarium

today?" Mia asked George urgently.

George looked around the room. "Does your armchair have caster wheels underneath?" he asked Grandpa Frank.

"No it doesn't. But I do believe there's a lady on the ground floor who has a wheelbarrow in her garden..."

"Too small and wobbly," Mia dismissed the idea.

"Wait!" George shouted enthusiastically, throwing his hands into the air. "I saw a supersized shopping trolley dumped behind a bush a little way down the street on my way here. He could definitely fit in that, if he just bends his tail upwards."

"Perfect!" Mia cried out joyfully.

"I'll go and get it!" George declared, and as he hurriedly left the apartment to complete his mission, he tapped himself on the back and muttered, "You're a genius Georgie-boy, a heaven-sent genius!"

Grandpa Frank shook his head in mock despair at his only son's antics, while Mia looked back at him and giggled.

George swiftly located the trolley, wheeled it to the entrance of the apartment block and wedged it behind an adjacent bush, out of sight. Mia padded it with spare pillows from her bedroom before she and George made sure the coast was clear and carried Mokoto down the stairs to put him in it. His long tail curved up and back on itself, so that the flukes were touching his chest, but he reassured them that it was bearable.

"We need a big blanket!" Mia declared, as she raced back upstairs.

"Grab one of Grandpa's t-shirts too!" George yelled after her.

When she rushed back down, her cheeks flushed with pink, she neatly arranged a large, floral quilt over Mokoto's tail, and tucked it in at the edges and at the end, while George helped him put the t-shirt on.

"I don't like it," Mokoto squirmed at the strange sensation of material against his skin. "It feels odd, like having lots of sea sponges on me..."

George and Mia were looking at his uncomfortable grimace

when the absurdity of the whole situation suddenly hit them. Here was a merman, stuffed in a shopping trolley, on a residential street, moaning about having to wear a t-shirt. They both burst out laughing to the point that George was wiping tears from his eyes.

"I don't understand what's so funny," Mokoto muttered sincerely, as he straightened out his long yellow locks.

"Here," Mia managed to utter, stifling her giggles, "let me tuck your hair behind your back. It's too eye-catching."

As Mia finished neatly arranging his golden mane, George took off his cap and placed it on Mokoto's head, suitably completing the look.

"You're good to go!" he told Mia and Mokoto with a grin.

"You're not coming with us?" Mia replied with concern.

"I wish I could, but I've got an extra tourist group booked in today so I've got to dash. Good luck you two, be as quick as you can and try not to draw too much attention to yourselves."

George pulled the trolley out from behind the bush and left it on the pavement, ready for Mia to take control. He then headed over to where his pick-up truck was parked, before looking back and shouting over, "I'll check up on Nui for you!"

"It's just you and me then," Mia sighed to Mokoto, and used all her might to push the heavy trolley forward as they headed into the day's adventure.

# CHAPTER 4

Mokoto was wide-eyed with wonder as he stared at cars hurtling along the streets and saw legpeople of all colours, shapes and sizes loitering and scurrying about. He gazed up at the tall buildings and down at the shop fronts, marvelling at this hectic, dry world and wondering just how long it must have taken for the legpeople to make it all.

He was too distracted by the sights and sounds, and Mia was too consumed by the difficulty of her task, to notice how many curious stares they were getting. Legpeople were pointing out to their companions the ridiculous man in the trolley, and at times, the traffic actually slowed down to take in the unusual scene.

They slowly bumped their way along to the dolphinarium and finally arrived at the ticket counter.

"Two please," Mia asked the cashier breathlessly.

The cashier eyed up Mokoto, who was still moving his head from side to side, glaring in astonishment at everything around him. The metal railings, the LED signs, the long buses chugging past. It was all so overwhelming.

"No trolleys allowed," she ordered sternly, making him jump out of his trance.

"I'm sorry," Mia replied, wishing she'd prepared herself better for this moment, "but my big brother's hurt his legs and this is the only way he can get around."

"Haven't you heard of a wheelchair?" the cashier huffed, unsympathetically.

"Yes, of course," Mia answered, trying to be careful not to stumble on her unrehearsed words, "the doctor said he'd have one available for him tomorrow. But he really wanted to come here today, because…because…it's his birthday."

Mia silently congratulated herself for her impromptu stroke of genius.

The cashier stared for a few more seconds then declared, with a frightening scowl, "Go on then, but only because I'm a nice person, and don't think you can ever try it again because I'll come down on you like a tonne of dirty bricks. Got it?"

"Got it," Mia confirmed, as the scary cashier handed over the tickets.

As Mia took them, she glanced to the right and noted a security guard in the glass walled office next door. He was sitting in a large, black swivel chair, eating chips and staring at a screen of CCTV images from around the complex on the desk in front of him. The office had its own street entrance and a back door leading directly into the dolphinarium, as well as a side door joining the cashier's area. The only CCTV camera she could see was one facing the cashier's till.

She didn't want to draw any suspicion by loitering for too long, however, so she quickly pushed the trolley down towards the pools. "We're in!" she cried out triumphantly, as they made their way along the interior pathway.

Mokoto, meanwhile, was grimacing at the overpowering smell of chlorine. "It's quite foul," he stated, as he popped his tongue in and out of his mouth, "I can even taste it in the air."

There was a dolphin show happening in the main pool, so Mia stopped the trolley right in front of the barrier at the edge of the water.

Mokoto's jaw dropped with dismay. "Look at how tiny the space is!" he cried out. "And look at the dolphins faces. They're so….sad!"

They watched the dolphins do forced dives, jumps and spins until the show finished and the crowds roared with delight before starting to disperse.

Mokoto took the opportunity to whisper in Dolphish, "I'm Mokoto, a merman from The Coral Kingdom. Has anyone seen my best friend Molailai and his family?"

However, none of the dolphins heard him over the sound of general chatter. So he repeated himself again, a little louder.

This time, the biggest dolphin shot her head up and turned to look at Mokoto, then sloped her way over to his side of the pool.

"Your friend is here," she answered hastily in Dolphish, knowing that her trainer would soon summon her back. "He's in a holding pool on the other side of this high fence," she pointed her nose towards a line of railings covered with fixed tarpaulin, "but there's a small gap between each railing, so you'll be able to see him."

"Thank you," Mokoto responded earnestly, "thank you so much."

"Anything to help a fellow sea creature," the dolphin replied kindly. "But please, please don't stay too long. If they find out what you are they'll imprison you too, and I wouldn't wish this life on anyone." Her spirit was clearly broken and she slipped away quietly back to the centre of the pool.

"She said he's over there," Mokoto told Mia. "Please take me to those railings!"

Mia looked serious and focused as she hurriedly pushed her merman friend over to the sheets of tarpaulin. She positioned the trolley sideways so that Mokoto could see through the divide and immediately heard him gasp with delight.

"He's there! I see him! And his mother! And his father! And his brothers and sisters! They're all there!"

"Can I see?" Mia asked gently, so Mokoto moved aside to let her look. There, Molailai and his family were crammed in a pool so small that they barely had space to swim. Mia looked back at Mokoto with sympathy, "This isn't fair. We've got to get them out of there."

Mokoto then peered through the gap again and called out to his friend in a series of whistles and squeaks. Molailai immediately recognised the sound of his best playmate and lifted his silky smooth nose in the air. When he eventually caught sight of his face through the fence, he screeched with happiness and flapped his flippers with excitement.

"Mokoto! You came for me! I can't believe it!" he sang out.

His family then joined in the jubilant chorus, "Mokoto's here! Mokoto's here to save us!"

The pool had erupted into an explosion of high-pitched trills and squeaks, letting Mokoto know how pleased the dolphins were to see him and how desperately they needed to get out of there.

"Don't make too much noise," Mokoto warned them, "or the legpeople will get suspicious. What are they planning to do with you?"

"The other dolphins say we'll be split up and sold to different dolphinariums," Molailai explained. "We won't see each other again. They'll probably keep two or three of us here to train and perform tricks in the bigger pool. They say they'll only give us food if we do what they want. The other dolphins are all so unhappy over there, they desperately miss their freedom and their families. And the water here hurts our eyes. We need to get back to the ocean, Mokoto. Please help us, Mokoto!"

"I will," Mokoto consoled him. "We'll be home again soon. I promise."

At that point, Mia felt an alarming tap on her shoulder and turned around to find a staff member in beige uniform glaring at her.

"All visitors are now requested to go to the information centre for a dolphin talk," she stated, with a notably fake smile.

"Okay," Mia answered, and smiled back but stayed right where she was.

"Now!" the staff member insisted, folding her arms in a determined stance. She clearly wasn't going anywhere until they'd moved on. So Mia reluctantly cut short the conversation between Mokoto and Molailai and shifted the trolley away from the fence.

They decided it was best to leave and start making a plan.

On the way to the exit, Mia told Mokoto, "You see those little black security cameras up there? They see everything that goes on in here and record it. Then the management can play it all back and watch it again. Try to count how many you can see around the place and where they're located."

"Wow!" Mokoto replied, "Really? They can do that?"

"Yes," Mia answered, as the enormity of the task ahead started to dawn on her, "and we have to try and remember the layout of this place…"

"Okay," Mokoto responded enthusiastically, starting to feel buoyed by Mia's determined demeanour.

As they exited the entrance area, Mokoto pressed Mia, "So when can we get him out of there? When it's dark? Tonight? How do you think we can do it? What about the cameras?"

"We have to be smart," Mia advised him, "and patient. We have to make sure our plan is perfect. Let's go home and figure it all out."

"Right," Mokoto agreed, "of course. But can we quickly visit a shop before we go back to the apartment?"

"I'm not so sure that's a good idea," Mia responded delicately.

"Please!" Mokoto begged. "No one in the dolphinarium guessed that I had a tail! We'll be fine! Just let me see all the food you can gather, at least!"

He had a doleful look in his big, blue eyes that reminded Mia of a puppy. She realised she didn't have the heart to refuse such an earnest request, so they meandered their way over to the supermarket.

As they entered the bakery section, with its mouth-wateringly appealing aroma, an assistant approached them with a tray of free taste testers.

"These are samples of our freshly baked bread rolls," she chirped enthusiastically. "Perfectly crunchy on the outside and beautifully soft in the middle. Please try one!"

Mia and Mokoto reached out at the same time and both groaned with satisfaction as the perfectly made, warm buns hit their taste buds.

"Exquisite!" Mokoto declared.

"Would you like a pack?" asked the sales assistant.

"Absolutely!" Mokoto replied, "We'll take two!"

They ambled over to the fruit and vegetable section, where Mokoto's eyes widened with delight at the shape and colours of all the unusual food on offer.

"Let's start gathering!" he told Mia. "Where's the green seaweed?"

"I don't think they have seaweed," she answered, "but you could try other green vegetables and see if you like them…"

"Over there!" Mokoto pointed to a shelf of broccoli, like a bold captain commandeering a ship.

He grabbed a handful and put it next to him in the trolley, then asked Mia to move slowly along the aisle, as he grabbed more handfuls of leeks, spring onions, lettuce, cabbage and asparagus.

He was like a child in a toy store for the first time, swooning over everything available and declaring his passionate enthusiasm for it all.

"It's so amazing that you have all of this in one place! So straightforward and easy! Can you take me to the strawberries please?"

"Sure!" Mia was riding the wave of his excitement and was quietly pleased that the land of the legpeople could offer something, at least, that impressed him.

He grabbed several boxes of strawberries and added them to his growing pile, then decided that it would be good to try other red berries too, so threw some raspberries and cranberries in for good measure.

"Is there anything else you think I should gather?" he asked Mia thoughtfully.

"Well there's a lot of other food that comes in boxes, jars and packets, but I think you should mainly stick to raw things, because that's what your body is used to," Mia advised, wisely.

Nevertheless, she pushed him through the rest of the supermarket, pointing out the various ingredients that she and her mother usually bought to make their meals.

As Mokoto reached out for a box of black tea bags, he finally remarked, "I think I've gathered enough now. Shall we go?"

"Okay," Mia agreed, then headed towards a cashier and waited in line.

"What's going on?" Mokoto whispered. "Why have we stopped?"

"Because we have to pay," Mia explained.

"Pay?" Mokoto was confused. "What with?"

"You can't just take the food for free," she told him, "you have to pay, with money."

"How do you get money?" Mokoto narrowed his eyes and tilted his head in bewilderment.

"By doing a job. My mom goes to work and gets money for it. I then do little jobs to help her at home, and she gives me pocket money…"

"But in The Coral Kingdom gathering food IS a job!" he shook his head at how ludicrous the legpeople's system appeared to him.

"Well that's just not how it works here. Everything in life is based on working to make money, then we spend it on what we need. If there was no money, nobody would bother working and nothing would get done. Nothing would be made. There'd be no services."

"There's no money in The Coral Kingdom and everything still gets done…" Mokoto enlightened her.

Mia pondered on what he had to say, before he continued, "But in any case, it all sounds totally confusing. And exhausting."

"I suppose it does," Mia sighed in agreement, "but I still have to pay for this with my pocket money."

"Thank you," Mokoto whispered sympathetically. "I hope you didn't have to work too hard for it."

# CHAPTER 5

The day seemed to be going smoothly, until Mia and Mokoto were waiting to cross a road on the way home. Then disaster struck.

The intersection was at the top of a hill, and on the corner there was a fishmongers, decorated with red and white striped awning. A group of smartly dressed ladies were chatting outside, close to where Mia was standing with the trolley, and the tallest one of them had a grey, long-haired dog on a leash.

"He's just so gorgeous!" one of the other ladies remarked about the pampered pooch. "How do you manage to keep his fur so sleek and shiny?"

"Fish," the tall lady answered, matter-of-factly. "A daily diet of raw fish, from this fishmonger right here. He can't get enough of it and wolfs them down whole in seconds. It's so cute!"

Mia and Mokoto could hear their conversation and Mokoto winced at the thought of this hairy beast chewing up his fellow sea creatures, munching on scales and bones.

The dog, meanwhile, had picked up on the slightest whiff of a familiar scent. Scales. Delicious, crunchy scales. He stared fixedly on Mokoto and then started tugging on his lead.

"Bailey! Stop!" the tall lady scolded him. "He's never usually like this!" she tried to convince the rest of the group, with a distinct air of embarrassment.

Bailey the dog then pulled harder and started barking at Mokoto.

"Stop it!" the lady commanded, "Why are you doing this?"

Mia and Mokoto were both desperately waiting for the lights to change so they could escape the obsessed hound. Mia felt a bead of sweat fall from her forehead as she alternately looked at the dog, and back at the light, then back to the dog again with sheer panic.

"Please change, please change..." she whispered repeatedly, as if the lights could hear her urgent pleas.

They didn't change in time, however, and before she knew it, the dog had thrust forward so fast it yanked the lead out of his owner's hand and lunged towards Mokoto.

Mia and Mokoto both screamed with fright as the dog jumped up and ripped the blanket away from Mokoto's tail in one fell swoop.

Two distinct gasps could be heard from the small circle of women. The first was when the dog leaped up to snatch the blanket, and the second, much louder gasp, was when Mokoto's splendid tail was revealed in all its glittering, colourful glory. Mokoto instinctively tried to cover it with his hands, but it was useless. His shimmering scales were on display for everyone to gawk at.

Mia then made what she will always remember as the biggest mistake of her young life. She let go of the trolley to try and wrestle the blanket out of the dog's mouth.

"Give it back!" she yelled angrily. "Let go, you naughty boy!" While his owner just looked on pathetically with both hands covering her open mouth.

Mia managed to yank the floral quilt from the dog's fierce grip, and only then realised that the trolley had started careering down the hill.

"Miaaa!" Mokoto howled hysterically, "Helllp!"

As he tried to twist his upper body around to look back, his cap came flying off and his long, yellow hair flew out behind him like flames from a rocket ship.

The trolley quickly gained momentum and there was nothing Mokoto could do to stop it.

"Ahhhhhh," he screamed frantically, as all hope seemed to fade, and he covered his head with his brown arms to brace himself for impact.

Mia took after him as fast she could, almost tripping over her own legs in the process, while a few onlookers on the opposite side of the road stopped to gawp at the bizarre situation.

It just so happened that the owner of the fishmongers was coming out of the hot pie shop, at the bottom of the hill, just as Mokoto sped towards him. With a flaky, pastry pie half stuffed in his enormous mouth, he put out both hands to stop the wayward trolley, then feasted his eyes on the contents.

"Thank you!" Mokoto cried out innocently, before Mia finally caught up with him and covered his tail again with the dog drool covered blanket.

"What have we got here?" the bald, red-faced fishmonger asked Mia as he wiped his hands on his apron.

"We're on our way to a fancy dress party," Mia blurted out quickly. She was getting good at on the spot cover ups.

"Now, I'm no fool," the fishmonger began, "despite what my mother used to say. And I know very well that..." he stopped briefly to lick the sweat off his upper lip. "....that is a merman! A proper, fully fledged, no bones about it, merman!"

"Well you're wrong!" Mia replied defiantly, "Now leave us alone!"

She hardly had time to catch her breath before she urgently turned around and angled her body so that she could use her full weight to push Mokoto back up the hill.

"I'm so sorry Mokoto!" she muttered, as she struggled to stop the tears from falling down her flushed cheeks. "I won't blame you if you never forgive me."

Mokoto was silent for a few seconds to regain his composure, before he finally responded, "I could forgive you of anything, Mia. It was just an accident. You thought you were doing the right thing. I know you have a good heart, and that seems to be a rare thing amongst legpeople. Besides, we merpeople have a saying, 'Without forgiveness there can be no love,' and we all need love; it's what keeps us going and makes life worth living. I think the same must be true for legpeople too, if you really think about it."

They were once again at the top of the hill, waiting for the lights to change.

"That's so beautiful, Mokoto," Mia managed to break a smile, "thank you."

When they arrived home, they saw George's pick-up truck parked on the street outside the apartment block. Mia then ran upstairs to get him so they could carry Mokoto up together.

"How did you get on?" George's broad grin beamed at them as he reached the doorstep, "Did you find him?"

"Yes," Mia and Mokoto replied in unison.

"And we're going to get him tomorrow night," Mia continued, "after we've devised the perfect plan."

"Well you can dolphinately count me in!" George happily put his hand in the air, "I love a good rescue mission!"

Mia rolled her eyes at her uncle's terrible sense of humour.

"DOLPHINately," he repeated, "do you get it? Do you?" He playfully poked Mokoto in the ribs.

"Yes!" Mokoto reluctantly replied as he shook his head at Mia.

"Well it'd be quite shellfish not to!" George proclaimed dramatically, belly laughing at his own joke. "SHELLFISH!" he repeated, "Do you get it?"

"Yes!" Mokoto and Mia shouted together, despairingly.

"Alright, alright!" he protested, "I'm not doing it on porpoise!...PORPOISE, do you..."

"Yes!" they cried out, "We get it!"

George was still chuckling as he lifted Mokoto's upper body out of the trolley. Mia grabbed hold of his tail and they made their way up to the fourth floor.

None of them had noticed the fishmonger peering around the corner at the end of the street. He'd secretly followed Mokoto and Mia home and was waiting to see which apartment window they appeared at. When he spied George's broad frame next to the curtains in the third apartment along, on the left side of the fourth floor, he started to devise a wicked plan of his own.

# CHAPTER 6

When Lana got home from work that evening and heard all about Mia and Mokoto's day, a mild sense of panic set in.

"This isn't good. We have to get him back out to sea as soon as possible. It's not safe for him to be here now that he's been seen."

Mokoto was back in his paddling pool with all of his gathered green vegetables and red fruit neatly arranged on a small plastic stool Mia had placed next to him.

He eagerly picked up the first one.

"Broccoli," Mia confirmed.

"Broccoli!" Mokoto repeated, "I even love the name! This is going to be delicious!"

He took a huge mouthful and his face suddenly screwed up in disgust as his cheeks faded to a pale shade of emerald.

"Disgusting!" he managed to splutter. "What do I do with it?" he begged, with his mouth still packed full of florets.

Mia ran off to get a small bucket.

"Here!" she placed it on his chest, "Spit it into this!"

Mokoto was deeply grateful and immediately emptied the contents of his mouth into it, while everyone cringed with exaggerated disgust.

"Charming!" Grandpa Frank joked.

"Okay," Mokoto shuddered, "I'll try again," and he picked up something else.

"Leek!" Mia announced.

Mokoto was a little more cautious this time, biting off just a small part of the greenest bit.

"Foul!" he grumbled incredulously, before spitting it out again. "How could anyone possibly think that tastes good?"

One by one, Mokoto went through all of his fruit and veg, repeating the same performance.

"It's all so horrific!" he moaned, "I never for a moment imagined it would taste so revolting."

"I could cook them for you," Lana suggested helpfully, "see if you prefer them that way? That's how we usually eat them, cooked."

"Thank you," Mokoto replied, "but I think I'll just stick to strawberries and tea from now on. And perhaps the occasional bread bun."

"Right, well I think it's time we had a family meeting anyway," Lana sounded serious. "Can everyone please gather around the paddling pool?"

George pulled Grandpa Frank's armchair over for him, and the rest of them sat on dining chairs, circling Mokoto.

"So," Lana began, "it's time to come up with an urgent plan. We need to brainstorm ways to get Molailai and his family out of that place…"

"We're one step ahead of you, Mum!" Mia interrupted proudly and went over to the desk to pick up a pile of printed sheets.

"These are aerial maps of the dolphinarium and the street that it's on," she told them, like a well prepared teacher.

"She's very e-fish-ent!" Mokoto joked to George, with his radiating smile.

"Whoo-hooo!" George responded triumphantly, "Learning from the master!"

Mia ignored them. "Mokoto and I have talked about it and decided that it'll be best to strike late tomorrow night, so we'll have time tomorrow to prepare."

Suddenly everyone looked solemn, as the seriousness of what they were about to do sank in.

"Mum," Mia looked up at Lana from her neat notes, "you're going to distract the security guard away from his office, just before Mokoto instructs the seagulls to cover all the CCTV cameras along the street and around the building."

"Right," Lana nodded, taking a deep breath.

"Uncle George, you're going to take Mokoto, and a ladder, into the dolphinarium and go over to the holding pool. Mokoto will get in the pool and lift each dolphin up to you. You'll take the dolphin over to the ladder and climb to the top of the wall with it."

"Woah, okay," George replied, reflecting on the enormity of his task. "Trespassing and theft," he added, "I better start working on my best look for my police mugshot."

"We're not going to get caught," Mia admonished him, "not if we stick to the plan."

"Where will you be?" Lana asked Mia.

"I'll be on the beach, on the other side of the dolphinarium wall. The sand there slopes down to the sea, so I'll lay some tarpaulin down and keep it slippery with buckets of water. Uncle George will lean over the top of the wall and drop the dolphin, so it slides down into the ocean. I'll then push it past the shallows so it doesn't get beached and then it can swim away."

"That's quite a high wall isn't it?" asked Lana with concern, "Won't the dolphins get hurt when George drops them?"

"They've got very thick skin," Mokoto reassured her, "and they often belly flop down onto the hard surface of the ocean when they're playing. It might be a bit uncomfortable, but they can bear it."

"Besides," Mia added, "we've got no choice. We've thought of every other possibility. I can't use a different ladder and carry the dolphins down because Mokoto says they'll be too big and heavy for me, and I can't swap places with mom and distract the guard, because the guard might think I'm too young to be out alone in the middle of the night and call the police."

"Mmmm..." everyone nodded in agreement as they considered Mia's argument.

"As long as Uncle George makes sure he drops them straight down onto their bellies, they should be okay," Mia tried her best to convince everyone.

"Grandpa Frank," Mia continued, "you'll wait in Uncle George's truck, which will be parked further down the street, and call Uncle George if you see anyone approaching the dolphinarium while he and Mokoto are inside."

"Aye aye Captain!" Grandpa Frank saluted his granddaughter, feeling genuinely impressed by her leadership skills.

"Here's a list of things you need to buy tomorrow Uncle George," Mia handed him a piece of paper.

"Three metres of thick, black material," George read out.

"I'll cut it into large squares for the seagulls to drop over the cameras," Mia explained.

"Right-ho," George agreed. "A long piece of tarpaulin," he read on. "No problem, they'll have it in the hardware store around the corner. A long black wig. Fine, they have them in the party shop. Bird seed, a puppy collar and a leash. Okay, they have them in the supermarket. Gloves with rubber grips. Ditto. A ladder and a big bucket. No need, I've got them already."

"Perfect!" Mia was satisfied that everyone had accepted their roles. "Any questions?"

Grandpa Frank put his hand up.

"Yes Grandpa?"

"What time will we go?"

"Two a.m." Mia stated, without hesitation. "No-one will be around at that time in the middle of the week. Plus there's a late night shop opposite that closes at one a.m."

"I go to bed at nine. Can I sleep first?" Grandpa Frank was thinking of his ageing energy levels.

"We'll all go to bed at our usual times and sleep first," Mia confirmed. "We don't want to risk feeling too tired and making clumsy mistakes. Uncle George can wake us all up as he's the biggest night owl out of everyone."

"True. Twit-twoo!" Uncle George tooted.

Mokoto looked puzzled, as he had no idea what an owl was, or why George resembled one, but he was learning to accept that there was a whole world of things he didn't understand about life in the land of the legpeople, and if he questioned everything then his new friends would end up spending every minute of their days explaining.

Lana was the next to put up her hand, "What are the wig and the dog things for?"

Mokoto flinched. He knew all too well what a dog was and it still made him shiver to think about it.

"For you," Mia told her. "You'll wear the wig and hold the lead when you knock on the security guard's door. You'll tell him that you've lost your puppy and ask him to help you find it."

"Genius!" George cried out, in support of Mia's cunning idea. He then shot his own hand in the air, "When will Mokoto get in the ocean?"

"He'll be too big for you to carry up the ladder by yourself," Mia replied sensibly. "Besides, it's too far for him to swim from here to The Coral Kingdom. Look what happened when he swam from there to here: he passed out with exhaustion from doing it."

Mokoto nodded in agreement. "We merpeople can't swim as far as whales and dolphins," he informed them. "Nui, my whale friend, migrates to different waters every year, she says it takes her about four full moons and she hardly eats anything on the way. She's pretty tough. And Molailai and his family often travel long distances. But the merpeople mainly stay in and around The Coral Kingdom and wait patiently for our friends to return. We don't usually swim a very long way, unless we want an adventure."

"We'll have to take him there in your boat, Uncle George," Mia clarified. "After we've released the dolphins, we'll drive around to the harbour and he'll show us the way from there."

"How will you even know the way, Mokoto?" Lana asked, totally intrigued.

"I just will. By the pattern of the stars, and the vibrations of the water and the sounds of the sea. But mostly by the magnetic field." There was a stunned silence and Mokoto sensed the family's bewilderment, so he decided to elaborate. "Each part of the ocean has its own magnetic signature," he explained, "which I can feel, and use as a map. It's like how sea turtles swim huge distances to return to the exact same beach where they were born to lay their own eggs when they're adults. They just know where to go because of the magnetic field. Like me."

The others all glared at him in fascination.

"Wow!" Mia exclaimed, "That's so cool! I wish humans had superpowers like that!"

"Maybe they used to," Mokoto considered, "when they had to do everything for themselves. But you've made your lives too easy now. You don't even need to travel anywhere to go gathering."

"Hang on," George was doing some calculations in his head, "how long is it going to take me to get you to The Coral Kingdom?"

"That I don't know," Mokoto shook his head. "All I do know is that I was swimming pretty fast when I came here, and it was night time when I left, and morning time when you found me."

"So it could take several hours…but I have to be back in the harbour by five thirty in the morning to take my customers whale watching. I've got a big group booked, I can't miss it."

"Okay," it was the first part of Mia's idea that wasn't going to go according to plan and she had to think on her feet. "We'll have to bring Mokoto back with us then, and take him earlier the next evening."

"I don't know," Lana shook her head with concern. "Spending one more day here is very risky. I don't have a good feeling about it."

"We don't have much choice though," George reasoned with her. "We'll just have to go with it."

"Alright," Lana reluctantly conceded.

"Right, if that concludes the meeting, then I'm off to bed," Grandpa Frank placed his hand on his back as he eased himself out of his armchair. "Good night all. Big day tomorrow."

When the others stood up too, Mokoto called to George, "Hey George, did you see Nui again today? Is she still there?"

"She's still there, waiting for you," George told him. "You know, Mokoto, it's in times of trouble that you realise who your true friends are. You're very lucky to have someone as loyal as Nui. It's not easy for her out there, she's getting boats coming up really close, making lots of noise around her, but she's sticking it out. All for you. She's a good buddy, Mokoto."

"I know she is," Mokoto answered sadly, desperately hoping that Nui would be safe for another two days.

"Don't worry, mer-guy," George leaned down and gave him a friendly pat on the shoulder. "You'll be reunited soon enough... having a whale of a time together!" He gave Mokoto a playful wink and Mokoto smiled back, feeling grateful for the kindness and loyalty of all his friends, old and new, from the land and the sea.

# CHAPTER 7

The next morning, Nui was headline news in the local newspaper. There was a photo of her mottled, bluish-grey skin partly showing above the water just outside the harbour, with a flurry of boats crowded around her and people clambering to film and take photos.

Grandpa Frank read out loud, "A group of marine biologists and other environmental experts will be holding a meeting today to discuss the blue whale's unusual behaviour and consider options."

"Consider options?" Mokoto repeated with horror. "What does that mean? What could they be thinking of doing with her?"

"Don't panic," Grandpa Frank tried to calm him down. "By the time they've agreed on a plan, you'll all be back where you belong."

"Besides," Mia added, "she's too big to take anywhere."

As the day wore on, there was a buzz of anticipation in the air as the family geared themselves up for their big rescue operation that night. Mia was sitting on the living room floor, cutting up the black material Uncle George had bought that morning into squares. He'd popped around after his early whale watching excursion just to drop it by, so Mia could get to work on it, then rushed back out again to get the other items on her list.

Grandpa Frank had dug out his old bird watching binoculars and was cleaning them in his armchair, ready for his surveillance role, and Mokoto was eating strawberries and daydreaming about the moment he'd finally be able to set Molailai free.

"You know dolphins usually swim hundreds of miles a day

in the wild," Grandpa Frank informed Mia as he rubbed the lenses. "Hundreds of miles in the glorious, open water. They must go crazy when they're stuck in a swimming pool. It'd be like keeping you or me in the bathroom for the rest of our lives."

"Or just in the bathtub," Mia added woefully.

A knock at the door jolted them out of their conversation and Mia cried out, "Who is it?"

"Me!" Uncle George called back. "With the rest of the supplies!" George had his own key to his sister's apartment, but rarely used it because he thought it was more respectful to knock when he knew someone was in.

Mia grinned as she ran to open the door.

"Great!" Mia smiled as she saw his shopping bags. "Can you put them on the dining table, please?"

Mia went ahead and cleared a space on the table and George's hands were full so he hadn't yet got around to closing the door of the apartment.

Within a few seconds, another figure appeared at the door, a person Grandpa Frank and George hadn't seen before, but who was scarily familiar to Mokoto and Mia.

Mokoto looked up and his blue eyes widened with shock as he let out a frightened whimper.

Mia gasped with terror as she immediately ran to Mokoto and protectively put her arms around his shoulders.

George raced back to the door and tried to close it, but the person standing there blocked it with his foot.

"What a sight!" the fishmonger declared in a scratchy, deep voice that sent shivers down Mia's spine. He squinted his eyes towards her and continued, "Just a fancy-dress costume was it? Does your friend always sit around in a paddling pool wearing his fancy dress clothes, does he?"

"Leave us alone!" Mia cried out, tightening her grip on Mokoto, "It's none of your business!"

"Please leave," George said firmly, as he tried again to shut the door, but the fishmonger stepped forward and blocked it again with his huge round belly, then forcefully grabbed it with his stubby fingers and pushed it further open.

"I'm not here to fight you," he rasped, shifting his eyes back and forth between George, right in front of him, and Mokoto, in the paddling pool. "Quite the opposite in fact. I'm here to talk business. Mind if I sit down?"

"Yes I do mind actually!" George shot back impatiently. "Get out!"

"I'm not going anywhere until you hear me out," their unwelcome visitor told them, before licking beads of agitated sweat off his stubbly upper lip.

"What you have here," he nodded towards Mokoto, "is a goldmine. And I can help you get your share of the wealth. I've already made a few phone calls and there are five-star restaurants all over the country who are willing to pay top dollar for genuine slices of merman meat."

Mia shrieked and drew Mokoto closer to her, while George recoiled in disgust.

"It's not as bad as it sounds," the fishmonger insisted. "You see, fish tails grow back, so I've no doubt your merman's tail will grow back too. We'll have a never ending supply. We only need to take fine slices to keep us in business."

Mokoto winced as his beautiful tail ached in protest at the very thought of it.

"I just need one small sample," the fishmonger pulled out a pair of tweezers and a small zip lock bag from the pocket of his apron, "for DNA, to prove to them that the meat isn't of any other known origin. Once it's confirmed, we'll be in the money! Discerning diners will be falling over themselves to try it!"

George was temporarily stunned into silence, so Grandpa Frank sat up in his armchair. "You're talking to the wrong people," he stated defiantly. "There's something called integrity that runs in our family. Look it up. It means we have firm principles and we always strive to do the right thing by each other and everyone else we come across in this crazy world. It's something you seem to be sorely lacking. Now get out of here, and don't ever think of coming back."

"You heard what he said," George tried to look menacing as he edged closer towards him, "Out!"

"You might want to take a bit more time to think about it," the obstinate fishmonger retaliated, "because one way or another, I'm getting my share of this pie." He paused to glare at Mokoto's stunning tail.

"Here's my number," he slipped a stained business card into the top pocket of George's short-sleeved shirt and tapped it twice. "If I don't hear from you by tomorrow night, I'm selling my story to the press. I have CCTV footage of what happened yesterday outside my shop. I bet the world would love to see it. So, whatever you decide, I'm making some money. Call me."

He raised his eyebrows in an expectant way, then licked his upper lip again before finally turning around and leaving.

George slammed the door shut behind him and held his head in despair.

"Please don't worry," Mia comforted Mokoto, "by tomorrow night you'll be out of here, and you'll never see that ghastly man again."

George and Mia then rushed over to the window to watch the frightful fishmonger plodding his way back down the street and make sure he wasn't still loitering outside their apartment. They both shuddered with disgust as they watched him stop to look at his reflection in a window and wipe his nose on his apron, then groaned with relief when he finally turned the corner at the end of the road and disappeared out of sight.

They were all clearly shaken up by the dreadful experience, but they mustered a fighting spirit and decided their only option was to channel their nerves into action. When Lana returned from work a short while later, they went over every last detail of their meticulous plan and made sure they were all aware of exactly what they needed to do.

At nine p.m., Grandpa announced that he was going to bed, so everyone else took it as their cue to try to get some rest too. Before George left, Lana asked him to make sure that he let himself into the apartment at one forty-five so they could all be ready to leave for their two a.m. start.

"Got it," George confirmed, in his dependable way. "You can count on me."

The lights went out and everywhere was quiet, but no one could sleep. They all tossed and turned as their hearts raced with nervous anticipation, tinged with jittery excitement. Their plan played out in their minds like movie scenes, while butterflies in their bellies fluttered uncontrollably, impatiently waiting for their bodies to spring into action.

Mia stared at her surfboard, resting against her bedroom wall, and thought about all the times she'd been surfing in the swell, oblivious to all the amazing and fascinating sea life beneath her. Sea life that had families, feelings and the ability to communicate. She'd never be able to think of the ocean in the same way again. She reflected on how amazing it felt to ride the waves, and how dolphins in the wild live that exhilarating reality every day, using the vast ocean as their endless playground.

By the time George came back, right on time, everyone heard the door key turning. Mokoto was sitting up straight in the paddling pool, wide awake, twiddling his thumbs, and the others were all out of their beds before George even had a chance to knock on their bedroom doors.

Lana set to work immediately, tucking her short, brown hair under the long, black wig and applying a full face of makeup that made her virtually unrecognisable. She then threw a big, brown cardigan over her striped pyjamas and was good to go.

"That's perfect," Mia gave her seal of approval, before checking with George that the ladder and bucket were in the truck.

Grandpa hung the binoculars around his neck and Mia clutched her bag full of black squares and watched while George and Lana lifted Mokoto out of the pool. They carried him downstairs as quietly as they could, with Mia and Grandpa Frank silently slipping out after them.

They laid Mokoto down in the tray of George's truck, next to the ladder, and covered him with the same blankets from the back seat that they'd used last time, so that only his face was showing.

Thankfully, no one had moved the trolley from behind the bush at the entrance to the apartment, so George then lifted that in too.

Grandpa Frank took his place in the front seat and Mia and Lana climbed into the back, before George took his place in the driver's seat and started the engine.

They were on their way.

# CHAPTER 8

George was taking deep breaths as he drove, trying but failing to calm himself for the task ahead. He was already wearing the gloves with rubber grips that he'd bought from the supermarket and was tightening and releasing his hold of the steering wheel, trying to focus on the odd sensation in his fingers to distract himself from his fast beating heart. Grandpa Frank was shaking the box of bird seed he was holding with jittery repetition and nervously tightening his grip on his walking stick with his other hand. Lana tapped her foot anxiously, furtively looking out of the window to see who was out and about at this time, while Mia bit her bottom lip and repeated in her head that everything was going to be okay.

None of them noticed any people on the pavements, which they all found reassuring, and the only traffic they passed was a street cleaning truck.

They pulled over at the very end of the long, palm tree lined road that the dolphinarium was on. Mia gave three, firm knocks on the glass window behind the back seats, letting Mokoto know, in the cargo tray behind, that it was time to summon the seagulls.

Mokoto sat upright and softly started making a cooing sound, moving his head from left to right as he looked around to try and sight their wingspans in the night sky.

When it was clear that none were appearing, his sounds progressed to louder, warbled screeching, which quickly did the trick. A flock of inquisitive gulls flew over the beachside buildings and gracefully glided down onto the side of the truck's tray, beside Mokoto.

Resting on their delicate legs, with their soft, white feathered bodies neatly standing next to each other, they eagerly waited to take their orders and follow instructions. As Mokoto looked along their line of yellow beaks, he was suddenly touched by their familiarity and loyalty, and it reminded him of how much he missed his life in the sea.

"I am Mokoto," he introduced himself in the garbled, warblish sounds of seagull squawks, "a merman from The Coral Kingdom. I need your help to rescue my dolphin friend and his family, who were kidnapped by legpeople and are being kept in the dolphinarium over there." The seagulls all craned their necks to look over in the direction of the dolphinarium and nodded to show that they knew the place.

"I've made friends with some kind legpeople," Mokoto continued, "and tonight we will release my friend, and the other dolphins, back into the ocean."

The seagulls all squawked their approval and lightly flapped their grey wings in support.

"What do you need us to do?" the seagull on the furthest corner of the tray screeched.

"Right," Mokoto sounded serious and the birds all put their heads forward to listen a little closer, "have you seen those little, black boxes at the top of long poles, in and around the dolphinarium?"

"Yes," the seagulls responded in unison.

"They're called cameras. They see everything and tell the legpeople what's happening. So we need to cover them, with these…"

He grabbed the bag of material and pulled out one of the black squares. "I need each of you to each take one and cover a camera with it. All the cameras have to be covered. The ones inside the dophinarium, the ones on the street outside it, and the ones facing the beach outside it."

Mokoto ran his eyes along the line of studious bird faces, who were jerking their heads in concentration. "Do you understand?" he asked, but he knew from their looks that these gulls were serious.

"Yes! Yes!" came a chorus of squawks.

"There are enough of you, and enough squares, to do it. You might even have extra. If you can't find a camera to put your square on, drop it back here in the tray of this truck."

"When do we start?" the fluffiest bird cooed.

"On my command," Mokoto told them, like an army general. "And when you've covered the cameras, you must stay close by, watching the truck. When we've finished rescuing the dolphins and I get back into it, I'll give you the go-ahead to pick up the square you left and bring it back to me. Is that clear?"

"Clear! Clear!" they warbled.

"I'm going to give you each a square now, but I don't want you to leave with it until I say so." He gently placed a square of black material into each of the bird's beaks and they dutifully held onto them.

"We're going to move the truck further down the street now, so we can see the entrance of the dolphinarium," he warned them. "So it's probably best if you fly off the tray and land back on it when we've stopped again."

The birds dutifully swarmed away in a mass flutter of wings and waited on a nearby wall, carrying the black squares in their beaks. Mokoto tapped the back window of the truck three times, signalling to George that it was time to start the engine again, and the truck moved forward.

When they caught sight of the entrance to the dolphinarium in the distance, George stopped again, outside the front of a graffiti covered, run down store that had closed down a long time ago. Mia's stomach lurched. This was really it: the moment they'd all been waiting for.

Mokoto cooed lightly again to call the birds back and they all faithfully returned to their previous positions around him.

"Here goes," Lana whispered, as she tensely tucked a few stray, brown hairs under her black wig with her trembling fingers. "Just remember everyone," she leaned forward to look at George, then back at Mia, "If you find yourself in any kind of trouble, just run. Run as fast as you can back to the truck. And I want you to know...I'm proud of you. I'm proud of all of us."

She opened the car door and stepped out, as George quietly called behind her, "Go get him, Lanie!"

"Go on, my girl," Grandpa Frank added, with a proud wink.

"You can do this Mum!" Mia was the last to add, before Lana gently closed the truck door.

"See you later, Mokoto," Lana breathed towards the tray, "and thank you seagulls."

"Good luck Lana!" Mokoto whispered back, but the seagulls had no idea what was being said and kept perfectly still and focused.

Lana began her act as she neared the entrance of the dolphinarium, holding the puppy collar and leash and frantically calling out the name, "Trixie! Trixie!" while bending down to look under parked cars. Her heart was racing when she finally knocked on the security guard's door.

The security guard had seen her before he heard the knock. His CCTV cameras had clocked the worried looking woman searching for her lost pet and he was already feeling sorry for her.

He put his bag of crisps down, quickly ran his fingers through his hair and checked himself in the mirror on the wall behind him, then opened the heavy door.

"Hello!" Lana cried out straight away, her innocent looking, flustered face seemingly wracked with distress. "I'm so sorry to trouble you, but I've lost my puppy!"

She tried her best to fake some tears, but unfortunately they wouldn't come, and she was left with screwed up, dry cheeks.

"It's okay Madam," the security guard tried to comfort her. "Where did you last see it?"

Lana pretended to sniff with upset. "I live a few streets away. She was crying in the night and woke me up. I thought she probably needed to go and pee, so I took her out. But she slipped out of her collar and ran away, down this street..."

"Uh-huh," the security guard narrowed his eyes as if he was listening attentively, but he was really wondering whether the woman wore that much makeup to bed, or whether she put it on just to take her puppy out for a walk.

"Can you help me find her, please?" she whimpered, trying her best to flutter her fake eyelashes, which made her look like she had something stuck in both eyes.

"Sure," the security guard agreed. His night shift at the dolphinarium was actually quite boring, and most nights he struggled to stay awake. He'd eat chips, play games on his phone and read the news, but it was always hard to fill those long, dark hours without feeling tired, so this woman's visit came as a welcome relief to his usual routine.

The security guard stepped out onto the street and reached for the cluster of keys attached to his belt strap. Just as he turned around to lock the door behind him, Lana cried out dramatically, "There she is! I just saw her! Running down there!" she pointed down the road, jabbing her finger frantically in the direction that they needed to go. So, instead of fully closing and locking the door, the security guard turned on his heels and ran off down the street, with Lana by his side.

As soon as George and Mia saw them heading away from the dolphinarium, they sprang into action, flinging open the truck doors and jumping out like an elite army team.

"Now!" Mokoto ordered the seagulls. "Go!"

In a scrambled flutter of wings, the seagulls all took off, racing through the dark night sky to complete their mission.

"Woah!" Mia exclaimed, as she looked up at the helpful flock of birds soaring towards the dolphinarium, impressed with how they'd totally understood Mokoto and were diligently doing their job.

"Eww!" Mokoto squealed at the same time, noticing a runny splodge of bird poop that one of the gulls had left behind on the side of the tray.

George swiftly lifted the trolley out and placed it on the pavement, before leaning in again and grabbing Mokoto under the arms so he could pull him out. "Get hold of his tail!" he told Mia, "Quickly!"

"Mind the bird poop!" Mokoto whispered in revulsion as they hauled his heavy body out of the truck, "Don't get it on me, please!"

They placed Mokoto in the trolley, so his tail bent back on itself and rested on his bare chest, but this time it wasn't as comfortable. They'd forgotten to pad it out with pillows and his back felt uncomfortable wedged against the hard, metal wire.

"The pillows! We forgot the pillows!" Mia cried out, looking at Mokoto sympathetically. "We could put some of the blankets from the tray down in it instead?" she suggested.

"They won't make much difference," Mokoto replied stoically. "Besides, it's not far. Let's just get on with it. It won't be that bad."

George then reached for the heavy ladder and set it down on top of Mokoto's tail and Mokoto silently groaned in pain as he supported it with his big hands.

Mia leant over the side of the tray and snatched the tarpaulin and the bucket. "I'm going to the beach," she informed them, buzzing with nervous energy.

"Right," George looked at her. "Just remember what your mum said, if you're in danger, run. And if you need me right away, just scream, I'll be able to hear you and I'll be right there."

Grandpa Frank poked his head through the open truck window and softly called out to her, "Just take care, little girl. Stay safe. Remember, you're my one and only grandchild."

"Don't worry, Grandpa," Mia hastily reassured him, before rushing off barefoot down the street, away from the dolphinarium.

"One of the greatest gifts I've ever had," Grandpa Frank muttered proudly, as he watched her fade into the distance and slip off into one of the palm-lined side roads, towards the beach.

"We're going," George told his father, "Keep a close eye on the entrance and call me if you see anyone."

"Message received and understood," Grandpa Frank gave him a reassuring nod, then watched through his binoculars as George rapidly pushed Mokoto down the street.

"Good luck my boy," he breathed to himself, "Get those dolphins back where they belong."

# CHAPTER 9

The security guard was on his hands and knees in the street, looking underneath cars.

"Trixie! Trixie!" Lana was calling out to her imaginary puppy.

"Trixie!" the security guard was repeating, "C'mon now, come back to your mummy, like a good girl."

"I think I saw her tail! Over there!" Lana cried out convincingly, drawing the security guard further down the road, away from the dolphinarium.

Meanwhile, Mia had reached the wall on the beach side of the dolphinarium and was beginning to level out bumps in the sand where she intended to lay the path of tarpaulin. She removed any large, hard stones and used her hands and bare feet to create a smooth track to the sea. She then set about unfolding the large piece of blue, waterproof cloth, and hastily laid it out so that one end touched the base of the wall and the other met the gentle waves as they lapped onto the shore. It seemed to glow beneath the moonlight, shining like a glimmering pathway to freedom, connecting the dry world to the wet.

"Perfect," she told herself, putting her hands on her waist as she inspected her work with a perfectionist's eye. She levelled out some more bumps and straightened some creases before bounding down to the edge of the water with her bucket, filling it up and pouring it onto the material, so that it was suitably slippery and ready to serve its purpose.

On the other side of the dolphinarium, George had nudged the security guard's door wide open with the trolley and had to position the ladder flat against Mokoto's squashed face so that it could fit through. Once they were inside the small office, the top of the ladder almost reached the ceiling, even at an angle, and the space felt uncomfortably tight.

George glanced at the computer screen and all he saw were black CCTV images, so he breathed a sigh of relief that the trusty seagulls had successfully done their job.

He squeezed himself around the trolley and went to open the door on the opposite side of the room, which led into the dolphinarium. It was locked. He was gripped with panic. "Think George, think!" he told himself, as he desperately tried to figure out where the key might be.

He thought back to when he saw Lana and the security guard leaving the office and remembered that he'd seen a big group of keys hanging from the security guard's belt.

"What if the security guard has the only key?" he asked Mokoto, as he looked all over the desk and opened the messy drawers to frantically rummage inside. He pulled out candy wrappers, chip packets, dirty tissues and old receipts, before agitatedly stuffing them all back inside.

"I found a baby crab with an injured claw once," Mokoto blurted out from behind the ladder rung that was resting on his cheek, "and I put it behind some sea lettuce to keep it safe. I think you should look behind that plant," he suggested, pointing towards a spiky cactus on a tiny shelf, the only flora that the security guard had managed to keep alive after all his years working in this lonely room.

George turned around and lifted up the plant pot when a silver key fell off the shelf and landed on the tiled floor. It was the most wondrous, metallic clinking sound he'd ever heard.

"You genius Mokoto!" George cheered, as he fumbled about trying to pick the key up with his gloved hands.

Once it was firmly in his grip, he slipped it into the lock and rejoiced when it turned.

"We're in!" he sang out, as his heart leaped with a mixture of joy and nerves and the smell of chlorine flooded into the room. He then tucked the key into the back pocket of his rolled-up jeans, mindful that he might need it again if the door locked shut behind them.

He hurriedly pushed Mokoto through and they dashed down the pathway, towards the main pool, before veering right, under Mokoto's instruction, to dip through a gap in the fencing around the holding pool.

As the trolley clattered over to the pool, Mokoto caught sight of Molailai right away, crammed in with the others and uncomfortably jammed against the side, with his long blue-grey nose bobbing up and down. He'd been keeping watch continuously since Mokoto's first visit, certain that his loyal friend would stay true to his word and come through for him. When he finally caught sight of him, they locked eyes and Molailai nodded his head up and down with overwhelming relief and gratitude. When the other dolphins saw him too, they all started to squeak with excitement and the small space of water became alive with frenzied splashes of water.

"We're getting you out of here!" Mokoto clicked and squealed in Dolphish, "But you have to do what we say. Please stay as still and as quiet as you can. It's very important."

The burst of commotion gradually subsided as the pool became calm once more.

"This is my friend. He's called George. He's a legperson, but he's a good one. You can trust him. He's going to put me in the water with you so I can lift you out, one by one, and pass you to him. Then he's going to carry you to the top of that wall over there," he pointed up to the tall barrier that separated the dolphinarium from the dolphin's natural home, "and drop you down on the other side."

A few more whistles erupted as a carpet of smooth, shiny heads bobbed up and down.

"When he drops you," he continued to whistle and squeak, "be sure to keep your belly down and your nose up. You'll land on a soft surface and slide into the sea. My girl leg-friend, who you saw me with yesterday, will be on the other side. She'll help push you into deeper water. Then, when she lets go, swim as fast as you can, back home."

Although silence had once again fallen on the pool, there was a buzz in the air that they could all feel. The energy was electric and George couldn't remember a time when he felt more purposeful, driven and alive.

"I know you're tightly packed in there, but please make a small space for me!" Mokoto told the excited group.

The dolphins obediently squeezed themselves even closer together.

"Let's do this!" Mokoto nodded towards George, who then pushed the trolley as close to the edge of the pool as he could, and with a concerted groan, heaved Mokoto out, so that his tail slapped against the concrete below, and dropped him into the water.

"Ow! My eyes!" Mokoto shrieked as he blinked furiously. "What do they put in this water? It's dreadful!"

"We're all hurting from it," Molailai sympathised. "I can't wait to get back into our salty home again."

"And have space again!" one of Molailai's brothers added eagerly.

"And play again!" his sister joined in.

"And spend time with my brothers and sisters again," Molailai's mother piped up with relief. "I was beginning to think I'd never see them again. Thank you for doing this, Mokoto." She gently nudged him with her nose and smiled.

"Anyone would do the same," Mokoto insisted. "I can't wait to get back there too, but I won't be joining you until tomorrow night. George will take me on his boat so I don't have to swim all that way. Please tell my family that I'm safe, I miss them and I'll see them very soon."

"We will, dear," Molailai's mother reassured him. "They won't have gone ahead with the Feast of Kalani without you. You have all that to look forward to on your return."

In the meantime, George had carried his extendable ladder over to the wall and was lengthening it and locking it into place. He then climbed up, taking sturdy, experienced steps that minimised any wobbling, and balanced at the top as he peered down to the other side of the wall.

There, he saw Mia, still methodically filling the bucket and wetting the tarpaulin while she waited for her uncle to appear.

The problem was, Mia had laid the path further along the wall, so George had to get down again and move the ladder along so that it was directly above it.

"Mia!" he hissed into the warm night air before he got down, "Up here!"

Mia was overjoyed to see George's broad, smiling face beaming down at her reassuringly from above. She waved back enthusiastically then gestured for him to move further along.

When George had moved the ladder to the perfect spot, the rescuing began. He hurried back to the side of the pool and told Mokoto, "Pass Molailai to me!"

"No," Mokoto answered back, "he's insisting on going last."

Molailai didn't want to leave the pool until he was sure that everyone else had successfully secured their freedom, so he floated steadfastly by his family's side, to watch them leave their prison.

Mokoto then went to pick up Molailai's mother. "No!" she desperately clicked back, "I have to make sure my children are safe first!"

So he reached out for Molailai's younger brother, who began to squeak, "No! I…"

"Someone's got to go first! And we're losing time!" Mokoto interrupted him as he lifted the adolescent dolphin out of the water.

George grabbed him from Mokoto and grasped him firmly with his gloves. He realised what a good idea it was of Mia's to insist on these rubber grip gloves, as the dolphins were slippery even in Mokoto's water wrinkled fingers.

He held the dolphin tightly across his chest, wrapped both arms around him, and charged over to the ladder. Climbing up was trickier than he imagined, with such a large mammal to hold. After a bit of grappling, he quickly realised it was best to position the dolphin's head over his right shoulder and hold his body upright against his own, with one strong arm, as if it was a child, then steady himself firmly on the ladder with his other hand.

The dolphin's little face peered out over the legman's broad back, his mouth turned down with worry. He didn't like being apart from his family and he knew that one small mistake could send him flying onto the hard concrete below.

When George reached the top, he pressed his upper body against the wall to keep himself stable, then brought both his hands up to hold the dolphin in the grip of his gloves again. This manoeuvre was the most difficult part so far and George suddenly felt terrified that he'd drop him. His heart was pounding and he felt beads of sweat trickling down into his eyes, but he couldn't wipe them away.

Once he'd steadied himself and was sure of his grasp, he leant over the top of the wall and lowered the dolphin as far as he could stretch.

Mia gasped loudly when she looked up and saw the dolphin dangling above her head, squirming with fright and letting out startled squeaks.

"Do it!" she yelled up to her uncle, eager to put the dolphin out of his misery as soon as possible.

She nervously braced herself for this first fall to freedom and waited with baited breath to watch her carefully planned dream turn into reality.

George grimaced with concern as he mustered up the courage to let go. It felt wrong to drop such a beautiful creature from such a great height, so he had to fight the force of his protective instinct to do what he knew was right. When he finally summoned the fortitude to release his grip, he turned his head away and let out a muffled shriek. He only managed to watch through the corner of his eyes because he was so scared about the whole thing ending in disaster.

The dolphin released one long, distressed squeal as he plunged through the air, wide-eyed with fright and tensely drawing back his flippers as he prepared himself for impact. Mia simultaneously screamed with nervous anticipation as she watched him drop down, like a terrified baby bird falling out of its nest.

Her shock soon turned to elation, however, when she saw him bump down directly onto his belly, just as she'd imagined, and slide down the slippery slope, nose-first, straight into the welcoming sea.

Mia briefly clapped her hands with joy and relief, then jubilantly raced down towards him. With one hand either side of his solid body, she immediately pushed him out of the shallows and marvelled at the feeling of his silky smooth, rubbery skin on her hands and arms.

She kept propelling him forward until she was waist high in water and her denim shorts were soaked. Then she stopped and let go of him.

"Go, go, go!" she shrieked urgently. "Get away from here and never come back!"

The dolphin stopped to look her in the eye, before turning his mouth up at the ends, jabbing his nose up into the air and squeaking at her. Mia didn't have to understand Dolphish to know that he was saying thank you, and a small lump appeared in her throat as she nodded in acceptance of his grateful gesture.

He then curved his way under the water and darted off under calming ripples of shimmering moonlight.

It was such a wonderful experience, Mia had to shake herself back into the moment and remind herself that she had to head back to the wall. This was just the beginning; her job was far from finished. She waded towards the sand and looked up to see George's face, still there at the top of the wall, staring at the free dolphin with a huge smile on his face.

"It worked!" he beamed at her with delight. "It really worked!"

"We have to be quicker than this!" Mia shouted back insistently. "As soon as you throw one down, run back to get another!"

"Yes, right..." George mumbled back as he started to clamber down the ladder in his damp clothes.

"He made it!" he whispered loudly to Mokoto as he bolted back to the pool, "He's fine! He's free!"

# CHAPTER 10

Mokoto was ready and waiting with another dolphin in his arms when George bounded back with the good news. He flashed his pearly, white teeth as he grinned with relief and reached up to hand George the next one.

George grabbed the dolphin in the same way as before and made a quicker dash up the ladder this time, feeling more certain and confident of his technique. Once again, he hesitated for a brief moment as he leaned over the top of the wall, dangling the dolphin high over the beach below, but he took a deep breath and trustingly let go of her smooth body. He even managed to watch straight on, with both eyes wide open, and as soon as he saw her bounce onto the blue tarpaulin he raced back down the ladder to grab another.

Mia repeated the same sequence and was touched when this dolphin seemed to squeak her appreciation in the same way as the first. As she watched her gracefully speed away into the ocean, however, she caught sight of the first one in the distance, his dorsal fin poking above the tranquil water, waiting.

"Go! Get out of here!" she whispered uselessly to herself.

By now, George was like a well-oiled machine. He'd mastered the best approach and was racing back and forth like an energetic dog that continuously fetches the ball for its owner.

By the time Mia had ushered the third dolphin out to sea, she could see that the second had joined the first, and two dorsal fins were bobbing in the moonlight, patiently waiting for the rest of their family to appear. The third dolphin conveyed her appreciation, like the others, and swiftly swam out to join her siblings. Mia realised that none of them was going to head out into the deeper ocean until they'd all grouped together. She admired their solidarity and knew that her family would do the same if they were in a similar situation.

At this stage, Lana and the security guard were ambling along, casually calling out for the imaginary puppy while engaging in a friendly conversation about their lives. Lana knew that the best way to avoid answering questions was to ask questions, so she listened attentively to a detailed history of this man's life. His name was Tomasi and he'd arrived in the country from a tiny South Pacific island when he was a two-year-old boy. His family struggled initially, but he and his four brothers and sisters were all raised to be honest and hard-working, so that they always had money in their pockets. His father had died while he was still quite young, so he gave part of his monthly pay cheque to his mother and looked after her as much as he could.

Lana began to feel overwhelmed with guilt. The more she got to know Tomasi, the more she liked him, and she felt bad for luring him away from his post under false pretenses. Part of her considered telling him the truth, but she quickly thought better of it.

"You know Lola," he began, because that was what she told him her name was, "it's been good talking to you, and I'm sorry I haven't been able to find your puppy, but I better get back now. I don't remember locking the door when I left so I'm a bit concerned I left it open."

"Oh no!" Lana protested with rising panic, "Please don't leave me here looking for her alone!"

Back in the dolphinarium, George had just dropped the second to last dolphin from the holding pool over the wall and rushed back to fetch Molailai. Instead, he found Mokoto reaching his arms up.

"What are you doing?" George asked, looking confused. "Hand me Molailai!"

"We've got to do the others first," Mokoto stated, matter-of-factly. "Molailai won't leave until everyone's out of here."

"The dolphins in the main pool?" George asked in disbelief,

"That's going to take forever!"

He was feeling tired and knew that Lana wouldn't be able to keep the security guard distracted for too much longer.

"George, please," Mokoto looked up to him with desperation in his blue eyes. "I know you've already done so much to help us, and I can't thank you enough, but under the sea we have a code of loyalty. It's all of us or none of us. I thought the plan all along was to rescue all the dolphins. We can't turn our backs on the others. After all they've been through, they deserve their freedom more than anyone."

"Wait," George knew Mokoto was making sense and realised that it would also play on his own conscience if they left the longer serving residents behind. "Let me quickly talk to Dad and make sure the coast is clear."

He pulled his phone out of his back pocket and called Grandpa Frank.

"Everything okay?" Grandpa Frank answered anxiously.

"Yeh, we've freed the dolphins from the holding pen. Do we have time to free the others too? Can you see Lana?"

"No sign of her yet," stated Grandpa Frank, peering through his binoculars, "but she could be back any minute now. You'd be risking it, time-wise."

George looked at Mokoto and Molailai's faces, pleading with their sad eyes.

"We're gonna do it," he confirmed.

"Well just be as fast as you can," Grandpa Frank advised him, with audible concern.

George put his phone back in his pocket while Grandpa Frank continued staking out the street, noting the flock of seagulls that had reassembled on the nearby walls, patiently waiting for Mokoto to return so they could retrieve the black squares.

George sprinted back over to the ladder and raced up to call out to Mia on the other side of the wall.

"We're gonna grab the ones in the main pool too!" he yelled.

"Okay," she approved of the plan, "but be quick!"

George came back down and ran over to Mokoto. He reached under his arms, and with a monstrous groan, heaved him out of the pool and lifted him into the trolley in one fell swoop, leaving Molailai alone in the small holding pool.

"You're strong!" Mokoto complimented him, "Are you sure you're not part merman?"

George jolted the trolley on its stubborn, uncoordinated wheels, back past the makeshift fence, to the main pool. He pulled up right beside it, took a deep breath and shrugged his shoulders, before lifting Mokoto out again and dropping him in the water.

The dolphins all started swimming towards him, whistling with intrigue.

"I'm here to return you to the ocean!" he promptly explained in Dolphish, already grabbing the nearest dolphin. "My friend's going to drop you down into the sea! Don't be scared! It's going to be okay!"

"I'm...I'm going to see my children again?" asked the dolphin with uncertainty as George took her into his capable arms.

"Yes!" Mokoto confirmed. "You're going to see everyone again! You're going home!"

George tore out of the area with the dolphin in his arms, past the fence and alongside the holding pool, then flew up the ladder as fast as his legs could carry him.

"I'm scared!" the dolphin muttered in Dolphish, as her body trembled, and George could feel her fear so he tried to soothe her with comforting words that she didn't understand.

As he dangled her at the top of the wall, she was too anxious to even make a sound, and as she fell, she closed her eyes and gave in to whatever fate faced her. When she bumped down onto the tarpaulin, slid forward and landed at Mia's feet, she tasted the salt water and felt it splash into her eyes. Happy memories of jumping and spinning in the open sea water with her devoted family flashed through her mind like snippets of an old photo album. Mia pushed her out into the deep water, but she was temporarily stunned by her new surroundings and didn't move.

The moment completely overwhelmed her.

As Mia gently stroked her to reassure her, she slowly blinked and recalled the feeling of being totally carefree, swimming for miles upon miles with her pod, thinking that her world was gloriously endless. She remembered the shoals of colourful fish who would weave around her as she expertly swerved through the water, the vibrant patchwork gardens of coral, the swaying seagrass and the intricate, swirling patterns of beautiful shells. She could barely believe all of that was going to be accessible to her again after so many years.

It was the whistling and squeaking from Molailai's family, further out at sea, that eventually coaxed her into the ocean. She gazed up at Mia with a mixture of sincere gratitude and disbelief, before slowly sloping off. The old but familiar sensations of the sea immediately enveloped her; the tastes, the sounds, the smell. She picked up speed, and soon after, she jumped with joy when she realised that this was really it: her days of unhappy confinement were over and she was back where she truly belonged. She dived back below the waves, then soared upwards with a gleeful spin, delightedly thrashing her tail in delight for her newfound, and wholly unexpected, freedom.

Mia was deeply touched by this dolphin's hesitancy and uncertainty. It was clear that her years in the dolphinarium had taken their toll on her spirit so it was especially enchanting to see her embrace the ocean again with such a wonderful display of happiness.

Before she knew it, however, George had dropped another dolphin down, so Mia quickly waded to the end of the tarpaulin to meet it.

Again, the dolphin seemed a little shell-shocked and stunned by the sudden turn of events and took a while to figure out where she should go. As soon as she started swimming towards the others, however, the welcome familiarity of the salty sea water gliding against her smooth body energised her and reminded her of her previous life as a free sea creature. She leaped into the warm air and dived towards her future with reignited enthusiasm.

As Mia gazed at the dolphin's welcome committee, patiently waiting out in the deep water to greet her, she saw a burst of water gush upwards from amongst the crowd of dorsal fins bobbing in the sea, rising high like a fountain in a lake.

"Nui!" she gasped, as her heart sang with happiness.

Nui had heard the commotion from the growing band of released dolphins vibrate through the ocean like a sweet symphony and she immediately powered through the water to join her sea friends. When they told her that Molailai would be joining them at any moment she thrashed her enormous tail about with delight.

"Careful Nui!" the dolphins chuckled, "You'll draw too much attention to us!"

Everything seemed to be going well, until George had just dropped the third dolphin from the top of the ladder. The phone in his back pocket started to ring and he fumbled to take it out with his wet, gloved hands while trying to keep his balance. He managed to answer it with his dry nose. It was an emergency call from Grandpa Frank.

"They're heading back!" Grandpa Frank breathed urgently. "You've got to get out of there!"

"We've still got five to go! And Molailai!" George panicked.

"You've gotta leave them!" yelled Grandpa Frank. "Tell Mia to run, then get you and Mokoto out of there! Now!"

# CHAPTER 11

George shouted down to Mia, "Pack it up and run! The guard's heading back!"

Mia jolted with shock and shouted, "What about Molailai?"

"I don't know, just go! Go!"

Mia hesitated for a couple of seconds because she knew Mokoto couldn't leave without his best friend, but she reluctantly responded to the urgency of the situation and hastily started to gather up the tarpaulin.

George made a split second decision to leave the ladder where it was and sped over to Mokoto.

"We've gotta go! The guard's coming back!" he shrieked breathlessly, before leaning down to lift him out.

Lana was on the street, near to the entrance of the dolphinarium, pleading with Tomasi the security guard not to go back.

"I'm going to be scared out here all alone!" she begged him, mindful of the fact that she hadn't received the confirmation call from George that the mission was complete. It was taking a lot longer than she expected and it was hard work trying to keep Tomasi away from his duty for so long.

"Please stay with me! Just five more minutes!" she whined. "I'll pay you!" she then added, out of sheer desperation.

Tomasi stopped dead in his tracks and turned towards her. "I don't want your money," he stated, sounding a little bit offended, which made Lana feel ashamed. "I helped you out of the goodness of my heart. Because I like helping people. I never expected anything in return and I'd never take it. But you have to understand, if someone's walking along the street and finds my door open, they could walk in and steal some expensive equipment. I can't risk that. I'll get fired."

"Look around!" Lana cried out, "There's no one around at this time. Just five more minutes, please!"

"I can't," Tomasi insisted, uncomfortably.

"Please!" Lana shrieked, then impulsively decided to throw herself to the ground with genuine exasperation. "I can't live without her!" she yelled dramatically, hanging her head down while she was on all fours and thumping the pavement. "And I can't look for her without you! All I'm asking for is five more minutes...please!"

She glared up at him with a pitiful look in her big, brown eyes, framed by her impossibly long, fake lashes. It was the best performance of her life.

Tomasi looked down at her with shock and bewilderment written across his face. He'd never come across such a desperate act for attention. She clearly needed help, in more ways than one.

"Alright Lola," he agreed. "Five more minutes."

Lana crawled over to his leg and hugged it.

"Thank you," she howled, "thank you! Let's go! Let's go and find my Trixie!"

"C'mon, get up," Tomasi gently offered his hand. "We'll get your puppy back, crazy lady."

Grandpa Frank was watching the theatrical scene through his binoculars and almost applauded when he saw the security guard turn around and head back down the street with his daughter.

He briskly picked up his phone and called George again.

"It doesn't matter," the remaining dolphins were in the middle of telling Mokoto, sadly. "At least the others got out, and it was a nice dream for us while it lasted. Please try and come back again!"

Mokoto could barely stand how admirably stoic they were being in the midst of their sorrow. "Molailai will have to come in the trolley with me!" he told George, unable to bear the thought of leaving without him. "We can drop him off somewhere further along the shore! Please say that's possible!" he pleaded, as George answered his phone.

"False alarm!" Grandpa Frank informed George. "They're heading away again!"

"It's back on!" George shouted rapturously as he shoved his phone back in his pocket. "Grab another dolphin, Mokoto, I'll be back in a moment!" Mokoto threw his head into his hands and closed his eyes with relief, before explaining to the remaining dolphins that the dream wasn't over after all.

George then sped over to the wall to shinny up the ladder again and yell out to Mia, just as she'd started to sprint away, "Put it back! We've got more time! I'm going to bring the rest over!"

Mia turned on her heels and sprang back into action immediately. She hated the idea of leaving five dolphins behind when their friends had already been rescued. She wasn't sure what they were planning to do about Molailai and her head was spinning with the thought of all the other dolphins who were waiting patiently in the sea for the rest of the group to arrive. So she felt like a huge weight had been lifted from her shoulders when she knew the plan was back on track.

She'd just finished laying the tarpaulin out, albeit a bit more messily than before, when George was back up the ladder with the next dolphin. "Here he comes!" he hollered down to her, before dropping him without even flinching and going back for the next one.

Freedom tasted even sweeter to these last dolphins, who'd almost had it cruelly snatched from them in the final minute, and it took them less time to adjust to the wild openness of the sea again. Mia loved every second of watching them embrace their new lives.

Soon the fourth came, then the fifth. George was like a character in a computer game, tearing up and down the ladder to score as many points as he could in the quickest possible time. When he was rushing over with the sixth dolphin, however, Mia had spotted a group of people with torchlights further down the beach, heading in her direction.

"Uncle George!" she cried out, just as the sixth had fallen on his belly. "There are people coming!"

George looked up the beach from his elevated position and saw them approaching. "They're a while back! We've still got time!"

He ran back for the seventh dolphin as fast as his legs could carry him. When he returned, Mia was looking and sounding increasingly perplexed.

"They're getting closer Uncle George!" she shouted anxiously, as George dropped the seventh.

"I'll be as quick as I can!" George assured her, barely stopping to make his latest drop.

The figures were now more clearly in her view. They were a group of security guards. She wasn't sure where they were from, but they were moving their torchlights around, looking as if they were on a mission and striding forward with purpose.

"Uncle George! They're really close now!" she whispered this time, fearful that her voice would carry in the breeze and the group would hear her, but George couldn't hear her either.

He soon bounded back with the eighth, and last, dolphin from the main pool and almost toppled off the ladder in his haste to get to the top.

He saw how close the group were and told Mia to leave as soon as she'd pushed the dolphin out to sea.

"What about Molailai?" she muttered nervously, so that George could barely hear her.

"I'll take him out in the trolley with George!" he whispered down to her. "We'll put him in the truck and drop him up shore!"

"No!" Mia insisted, speaking as quickly as possible, so that the words were almost spilling out of her mouth faster than she could think about them. "The other dolphins are all waiting for him out there, and if these people see all those fins they might send for boats to get them! We don't know who they are or what they could do! We need to make sure all the dolphins leave, now!"

"Oh Mia," George sighed when he realised his stubborn niece wasn't going to give in. "Quickly then, get this one out there!"

He dropped the eighth dolphin then dashed towards the holding pool to get Molailai, while Mokoto was still in the main pool.

Mokoto had told Molailai that he'd be the one to lift him out of the pool, so when George came without him, Molailai was a little unsure about what to do and didn't immediately come to him.

"Please swim to me Molailai!" George pleaded on his knees in a language that Molailai didn't understand. "Mia's in danger! You must come now!" Molailai twisted his head in confusion, trying his best to read the situation. He then recognised George's beckoning hand gestures, from when Mokoto often motioned him to come towards him, so he decided to sidle over to the legman.

George grabbed him and jumped back onto his feet. He quickly realised how much easier it was when Mokoto handed the dolphins over to him. He then sprinted to the ladder and shot his way up in his fastest ever time.

"They're almost here!" Mia urgently muttered under her breath, genuinely afraid that they could clearly hear her now.

"Push Molailai out and run, Mia!" he instructed her as he dropped Molailai.

Molailai landed gracefully and glided down towards the sea while George continued to tell Mia, frantically, "Just leave the bucket and tarpaulin and run!"

He then took a few steps down and jumped the remaining distance off the ladder before swiftly collapsing it and carrying it under one arm as he raced back to Mokoto in the main pool.

Molailai had begun to sense the anxiety in the air so he quickly squeaked his thanks, in the same way as the rest of his family members, and affectionately nudged Mia's legs with his long nose before swimming back towards the others with effortless speed.

"You're amazing," Mia whispered quietly, feeling irritated that the group with torchlights had distracted her from enjoying the full majesty of this momentous occasion. It was the moment that she'd been imagining in minute detail from the second she and Mokoto hatched their elaborate plan. She wanted to linger and watch Molailai disappear into the peaceful horizon. Instead, she promptly glanced back and noticed with alarm that the unwelcome light bearers were nearing the wall.

She rushed out of the sea but was too much of a perfectionist to heed her uncle's instructions and abandon the bucket and tarpaulin. She didn't want to leave any trace of her actions, so she bent down to rapidly gather up the large expanse of material while keeping a skittish eye on the approaching group.

"Hey!" a man's voice bellowed from behind the advancing torchlight. "Who are you? What are you doing?"

Mia scrambled to grab the last bit of tarpaulin, stuffed it in the bucket, then ran as if her life depended on it.

"Stop right there!" the voice called after her, as she heard a mass of feet thundering along the sand, chasing her. Their heavy footsteps vibrated through her body and urged it to move faster.

She didn't dare look back and just kept willing herself away from the group, directing every last bit of energy into her legs so they continuously propelled her forward.

Holding the heavy bucket of tarpaulin tightly to her chest, she refused to let it slow her down and urged her long limbs to keep moving. She was like a gazelle being hounded by an ambush of tigers. They were relentless in their pursuit, but she was small, quick and nimble in her desire to escape.

They seemed to pick up speed and she began to imagine the scream she'd have to let out to summon Uncle George once she was apprehended. She knew he'd have to abandon Mokoto to get to her, though, so she somehow managed to muster extra strength and stamina to accelerate her pace and felt a welcome burst of power surge through her body.

She could hear the group huffing and puffing and knew that they were slowing down, whereas she was keeping up an incredible stride. When she felt that she'd put some distance between herself and the persistent pack of pursuers, she noticed an old, wooden rowing boat emerge through the darkness up ahead, leaning against a wall. She quickly and skilfully side-stepped to dodge behind it, and waited in silence, aware only of her quick breathing and the muffled sounds of the group in the distance.

She listened anxiously as their voices got closer. They seemed to have eased into a jogging pace.

"Was it a girl or a boy?" one of them asked.

"I dunno," a female voice replied, breathlessly.

"A boy I think, with long hair," another added. "Clearly up to no good."

They were right outside the boat now and Mia could hear their voices loudly and clearly. Crouching down fearfully, she tried to hold her breath so that they wouldn't hear her and bit her bottom lip as she waited for them to pass.

"Let's go up to the boardwalk," she heard a rousing voice encourage the others. "He must've gone up there. We'll find him."

Their footsteps and voices faded into the distance as Mia's breathing slowly and steadily returned to its normal rhythm. She just wasn't sure now how long she should stay in her hiding place and when it would be safe to leave.

# CHAPTER 12

In their hasty bid to leave the dolphinarium as swiftly as they could, both George and Mia missed the moment when Molailai's robust, streamlined body finally reached the throng of fins lingering in the water. He was the last to arrive and was greeted like a hero by the happy crowd.

Nui was the first to lurch over to him and Molailai instantly slid his head against his friend's enormous frame in a warm embrace. Nui then dived beneath him and surged upwards, sending Molailai soaring towards the surface and rolling about with joy, tumbling along Nui's back before playfully dipping down and prodding her belly from underneath.

"I was waiting for you and Mokoto!" Nui boomed gleefully to her energetic friend.

"Thank you Nui!" Molailai rubbed his face against hers.

"Is Mokoto on his way?" Nui's deep calls filled the water with cheerful vibrations.

"No, he's not coming until tomorrow night. His leg-friend is going to bring him on a boat. I'll tell his mum when we get back."

"Come on you two," Molailai's mother smiled at them, "we have to get out of here. The legpeople's world is no place for sea creatures like us."

"I have to wait for Mokoto," Nui told her friend.

"And I'll wait with you," Molailai confirmed.

"Molailai!" his mother scolded him. "That's madness! There are no dolphins left in that hideous place. As soon as they see you, they'll want to take you right back there! I know we should all wait for him, that's the way we always do things, but on this occasion we simply can't. He came all the way to the land of the legpeople to save us. He wouldn't want any of us to risk being trapped again and taken back there. It would be letting him down. We'll go and help the merpeople prepare for the Feast of Kai Kalani and welcome Mokoto home with a big celebration. Come on now, my son."

"She's right," Nui agreed. "I'll accompany you and then come back."

Molailai knew that he couldn't refuse his mother's request and was heartened that he got to spend a bit of extra time with Nui.

"Okay," he agreed. "Let's go!"

With that, the water exploded into a stunning blast of white water spray, as a flurry of tails splashed in the ocean and the merry group of free dolphins curved away from the land and towards the radiant moon on the horizon.

Their sleek backs effortlessly arced in unison, with their fins looping above and below the warm sea, as they travelled as a united team. By their side was their ever faithful, giant friend, Nui, who torpedoed along right next to them, riding high on the feeling of being reunited with one of her closest buddies.

It didn't take long for them to be totally out of sight of anyone on the land, as they dipped and dived under the stars and rapidly navigated their way closer towards the familiarity of home.

In the meantime, George and Mokoto were the only ones left in the dolphinarium and it had an almost eerie feeling of emptiness. The place that had housed so much unhappiness now appeared to be mourning its loss, bringing a still, sinister feeling to the air.

"Let's get out of here," George whispered with urgency as he bent down towards the main pool to hoist Mokoto out. "There's a group of security guards on the beach. They saw Mia."

"Is she alright?" Mokoto looked distraught.

"I told her to leave everything and run. She'll be fine. She's the fastest runner I know. But she'll be making her way to the truck and we need to be there."

When Mokoto's wet body was back in the trolley, George hurriedly placed the ladder back on top of him then rattled and clattered his way back towards the security guard's door, leaving a trail of drips from the pool to the office.

George tried to push the door open, only to realise that it must have slammed shut and automatically locked when they came in.

"I'm not just a handsome face!" George raised his eyebrows at Mokoto as he reached for the key in his back pocket and held it in the air like a shining beacon of liberty.

He briskly unlocked the door and wedged the trolley back into the small room. The door slammed behind him as he reached for the cactus plant on the tiny shelf and put the key back under it. He then squeezed past the trolley and rushed over to the opposite door. He gingerly poked his head out, quickly looking left and right, before being satisfied that the coast was clear and ramming the trolley back through the door and out onto the street.

"Ouch!" Mokoto cried in pain, as his back and tail forcefully pressed against the hard wire and a ladder rung banged into his delicate nose.

George barely registered his protest though. He had adrenalin soaring through every part of his body as his mind focused on successfully reaching the end of his mission. This was his last sprint to victory, the final leg, and he wanted to bolt towards the finish line as quickly as he could.

As soon as Grandpa Frank spied George and Mokoto through his binoculars, frantically bumping along the street as Mokoto winced in pain, he called Lana.

"Mission complete!" he confirmed with elation, before she'd even said hello. "Head back to the truck!"

"Yes!" Lana screamed out rapturously as soon as she heard the news.

Tomasi the security guard was once again on his hands and knees looking under parked cars for the fake, missing puppy.

"Who was that?" he peered up at her.

She hesitated momentarily before her jumbled mind tried

to think about what piece of information would convincingly fit in the jigsaw puzzle.

"The police!" she lied. "Someone's handed Trixie in at the police station!"

Lana looked at Tomasi's blank face and felt concerned that his mind was trying to figure out the details.

"My number was on her microchip!" she added, trying to make herself sound more believable as she turned away from him and started to briskly walk away.

Tomasi continued to look a little puzzled. The police station was a few streets away, and she was heading in the wrong direction.

"I've got to go!" she turned her head back towards him as she raised her hand in the air to wave farewell, without giving him a chance to ask questions or say goodbye. "Thank you for your help Tomasi! You're one in a million!"

He then watched as she fled back up the street, with her long cardigan flying out behind her, occasionally looking back to make sure that he wasn't following her.

As she hurried off, Tomasi stared at her departing frame in amazement. She was a mad mess of makeup, false lashes, impossibly long hair and pyjamas, but he actually quite liked her, and now their interaction had come to an abrupt end he found himself feeling a bit deflated.

He slowly picked himself up, brushed himself down and ambled his way back to his office to get on with his boring job.

At the other end of the street, George stopped the trolley next to the truck and bent over to catch his breath. The seagulls were all on high alert as they twitched their necks to watch Mokoto being pushed along the street and waited with focused anticipation for him to give the command to retrieve the black squares.

Mokoto's face was still uncomfortably squashed against the ladder, but from beneath the rungs, he let out a series of warbled coos and squawks that sent the birds on their way, and Grandpa Frank watched in awe as a mass of dutiful wings once again filled the evening sky.

Just then, Grandpa Frank's binoculars focused on Lana, dashing down the street towards them. She had the collar and lead in one hand while the other pressed down on top of her wig to keep it in place as she ran.

George glanced through the back windows. "Where's Mia?" he asked with immediate concern.

"She's not back yet," Grandpa Frank clarified.

"She should be!" George yelled out urgently, with rising panic sweeping his body.

"Mia! Mia!" he paced the pavement like a caged lion as his mind raced with what he should do.

By this time, Lana had reached the truck and flung open the back door to climb inside.

"Where's Mia?" she screamed out in distress, as she looked at the ominously empty spot beside her.

The seagulls then started to swoop back to the truck, dropping the black squares of material from their beaks into the tray and looking to Mokoto for acknowledgement of a job well done.

"I'm gonna go and find her!" George told the others, as he began to take off down the street.

"George!" Grandpa Frank called out to him, "Stop! It'll be quicker if we go in the truck!"

George paused and placed one hand on his waist and one on his forehead as he struggled to think about which option would be better.

"Let's get Mokoto back in and go," Lana sealed the decision and leaped back out of the truck.

George hastily lifted the ladder and placed it back in the cargo tray, revealing a red pressure mark across Mokoto's cheek, then heaved Mokoto out of the trolley. Lana carried the weight of his tail, and together they dropped him back in the tray, on top of all the black squares.

Mokoto then squawked a few notes of appreciation to the seagulls, who were variously gathered on nearby walls and railings, and told them that their heroic actions had helped save many dolphins. They ruffled their feathers with pride, satisfied that they'd carried out their task to the best of their abilities.

"Give them the bird seed!" he called out to remind Grandpa Frank, knocking on the back window and gesturing with his hands.

While George lifted the trolley into the truck, Grandpa Frank leaned through his window and emptied the contents of the bird seed box onto the pavement beside him. The birds quickly swooped towards it in a hurry, squawking with contentment as they furiously pecked at the welcome treat.

George then hurled himself into the driver's seat, started the engine, and briskly did a U-turn to go the opposite way down the street, towards the side road that Mia had taken to get to the beach.

Mia was still under the wooden boat, petrified of leaving at the wrong time and being caught by the group of security guards who were searching for her. She knew her family would be waiting for her, however, so she finally summoned up the courage to peek out from beneath the old, hollow cavity. The beach was empty and all she could hear was the familiar and soothing rhythm of mellow waves greeting the shoreline. She grabbed her bucket and quickly made a run for it.

She sprinted up to the boardwalk, to make her way down the side road, when she suddenly heard a voice in the distance bawling out, "There he is!"

Her heart jumped into her throat as she realised that they were still on her case, and she flinched with each thud of their determined feet that echoed behind her.

She quickly leaped over a low wall and raced along the pathway, still clutching the bucket full of tarpaulin, then darted left into the side road.

There, heading towards her, was Uncle George's white truck. Mia had never felt such an overwhelming sense of relief. She put her head down and ran forward with all her might. George sped towards her and promptly pulled a U-turn, screeching up beside her.

Lana leaned over the back seat to push open the door and Mia threw herself inside. George then floored the accelerator and the truck shot off, down the road and back onto the main street.

Half a minute later, the security guards turned the corner into the same road, agitatedly shining their torchlights, but their suspect had disappeared and they were exhausted, so they finally shook their heads and conceded defeat.

Lana wrapped Mia in her arms and held her tightly, while Mia soaked up the reassuring feeling of support and safety.

"You okay kiddo?" Grandpa Frank turned to look back at her.

"I'm fine," she reassured them. "It'd take more than a bunch of security guards with torchlights to catch me!"

# CHAPTER 13

There was a powerful sense of relief in the pick-up truck. Relief that Mia was okay, relief that they'd managed to get all the dolphins out to sea without being caught and relief that they were finally heading home.

They stopped outside the apartment and George carried Mokoto upstairs with Lana, then wedged the trolley behind the unkempt bush next to the entrance. It had been such a useful vehicle to move Mokoto around in, but he deeply hoped that they wouldn't be needing it again.

George was a well-built, fit and healthy man, but he was exhausted from his busy evening. His arms and shoulders ached and he felt an insistent weight pulling his eyelids down, so when he returned to his own apartment, close to the harbour, he immediately lay down and grabbed an hour of sleep before his early morning whale watching expedition.

Mokoto slipped under the water in the paddling pool and closed his eyes as soon as he was placed in there. Mia peeled off her wet clothes to change into her nightwear and jumped straight into bed, while Grandpa Frank and Lana didn't even have the energy to undress, and fell into a heavy, dreamless slumber as soon as they were horizontal.

Even the shrill sound of Lana's alarm clock at seven a.m. didn't wake the others. Lana objected to the rude reminder that normal life needed to resume and sleepily slapped her hand around on her bedside table in a drowsy attempt to turn it off. She could barely think straight, she was so exhausted. Her bleary eyes struggled to focus on the bathroom mirror as she peeled off the fake eyelashes and attempted to scrub the thick layers of makeup off her face.

She managed to drag herself out of the door to get to work on time, and left the others sleeping soundly.

They were finally woken by George, banging on the door, coming to visit, as he usually did, after his first whale watching trip of the day. Mia yawned and rubbed her eyes as she lumbered over to let him in. Grandpa Frank slowly pushed his blankets off, grabbed his walking stick and limped over to his armchair in the living room, while Mokoto eased his upper body to sit upright in his paddling pool.

Mia was only half awake when she released the latch but was jolted into full awareness as soon as she opened the door. She quickly recoiled in shock.

"What's your name?" a voice shrieked wildly.

"Where is he now? Can you show us?" another screeched.

George was standing in the door frame, and behind him, a sea of people, cameras and microphones were trying to surge into the apartment. He used his thick arms as barriers to try and hold them back, but they were pushing the cameras above his shoulders and through the gaps by his side, fiercely scrambling to get any shot of the inside of the apartment.

Bright lights flashed into Mia's face as she tried to shield her unprepared eyes and the shouting was relentless.

"How long have you had him?"

"Where did you find him?"

"Where are you keeping him? Can you show us?"

"Let me in, quick!" George yelled, doing his best to hold back the crowd. Mia stepped aside, and as soon as George was inside, they both used their weight against the door to forcefully slam it shut.

"What's going on out there?" Grandpa Frank croaked in alarm.

"Take a look at this!" George thrust the morning paper towards him.

Mokoto was headline news.

When the fishmonger had left their apartment the

previous day, he reflected on the reaction he got from Mia's family. The conversation hadn't turned out as he'd imagined and he rapidly lost hope that they'd take him up on his proposal. The idea seemed completely straight forward to him and he simply couldn't understand why they seemed so vehemently opposed to it. That evening, as he trudged down to the harbour to meet the returning fishing vessels and choose the best catch of the day, he saw the boat of his dreams for sale. He gazed longingly at its gleaming white edges and sleek lines and knew that it wouldn't stay on the market for long. He decided then and there that he needed ready cash more than he wanted some extra, long-term income. So, as soon as he'd taken his choice of fish, lobsters and crabs back to his shop, he headed straight over to the head office of the main television news channel.

When he produced his CCTV footage of Mokoto in the trolley, the Director's eyes widened with intrigue. He eagerly stared at the aggressive dog snatching Mokoto's blanket, then watched in awe as the shocking film clearly showed Mokoto's long tail being revealed, protruding from the trolley in all its sparkling, scaled glory. When he saw the strapping merman career down the hill, with his long, yellow hair flying out behind him, he knew it was going to be sensational news.

"I've got to have this!" he announced, slapping his hands together and rubbing them enthusiastically. "How much do you want for it?"

The fishmonger considered the cost of the boat he wanted and factored in some extra cash for incidentals, before he named his price. After a short round of negotiations, they settled on a sum and he happily gave the address where the merman was being kept. Soon after, he was walking out of the building with a healthy cheque stuffed into the pocket of his filthy apron, licking his sweaty upper lip as he quietly congratulated himself.

Later that night, it was broadcast as breaking news and the story was quickly picked up by other channels and newspapers. Every journalist in town wanted to investigate.

The first group of reporters arrived at the apartment

building shortly after Lana had left for work, and were swiftly followed by more. By the time George had arrived at his sister's home, the fishmonger had already cashed the cheque, paid for the boat and was sailing out to sea for the day in celebration of his success.

Grandpa Frank glared at the newspaper in disbelief. A huge photo of Mokoto in the trolley took up most of the front page. It was a still image from the CCTV footage, taken at the moment the dog had just pulled away the blanket. It showed the canine mid-action; his muscly, front paws high up off the ground as he gripped the quilt between his sharp teeth, leaving a stream of his spittle suspended in motion. Mokoto's fearful face was contorted with shock and his outstretched arms were half way to reaching for his tail in a futile attempt to cover it. Meanwhile, Mia had one hand stretched out towards the blanket in that fateful moment before she moved her other hand away from the trolley.

"Oh no!" Grandpa Frank sighed, shaking his head at the image.

Mia was perched on the arm of her grandfather's chair.

"Can I show Mokoto please?" she asked, before taking the paper over to him.

"Oh wow!" Mokoto muttered. He was less concerned about being revealed to the world and more astonished by the actual image. "That's me!"

"It must be the first time he's seen his own picture," Mia whispered sweetly to her uncle and grandfather.

Mokoto couldn't take his eyes off himself. He was astounded. His arms looked so firm and muscular, his cheekbones so chiselled, and he couldn't help but admire his perfect body-to-tail proportions.

George soon grabbed the newspaper out of his clutches and handed it back to Grandpa Frank.

"And look at page two..." he told him.

Grandpa Frank pulled back the first page to find the next big headline: Dolphins Stolen From Dolphinarium: Police Investigation Underway.

"Stolen?!" Mia cried out in protest, "That makes it sound so bad! We were just putting them back after they were stolen from the sea!"

"It'll fizzle out," George tried to reassure her. "They've got nothing on us. We didn't leave a trace."

Mia thought about how pleased she was that she hadn't left the bucket and tarpaulin behind. There weren't too many places that sold that brand of tarpaulin in town and it would only take a quick check to find out who'd bought it recently to lead them back to Uncle George.

"Check out page three..." George urged his father, so Grandpa Frank's gaze shifted to the next page.

"Resident whale finally leaves harbour," he read out.

It would have taken a very sharp detective to figure out that all three incidents were threads in the same ocean tapestry; a colourful sea story that had all begun with Molailai's disappearance.

"I saw Nui with the dolphins last night!" Mia shrieked. "She must have left with Molailai!" She turned to look at Mokoto, who'd only just shaken himself out of his stunned daze.

"Oh good," he responded with relief, "it's better that she's back home. Safely away from all the legpeople. No offence. But you know what I mean: the hideous ones."

"I know what you mean," Mia chuckled.

"Now go to page four," George insisted.

"Is this ever going to end?" Grandpa Frank sang out in despair, "Or is every news item in here connected to us? I'm not sure my old heart can take it!"

He gingerly turned the next page and George pointed to another headline.

"Thieves make off with designer pool mattresses from Excelsior Hotel," he read aloud, with confusion. "What's that got to do with us?"

"Read on," George encouraged him.

"A gang of thieves targeted the pool area of the beachfront Excelsior Hotel at around two thirty a.m. this morning and stole a pile of new, designer pool mattresses. Security guards were alerted to the robbery by a couple of startled guests who were going for a late-night swim. After combing the area, they narrowly missed apprehending one of the perpetrators but all, at present, remain at large."

"Those security guards…they thought I was one of the thieves!" Mia exclaimed.

"You were lucky to get away," Grandpa Frank muttered, then shuddered as he thought back to the moment they'd found her fleeing down the road to escape her pursuers.

George took a deep breath and let out a small whistle of air. "Well we've done what we needed to do, and that's all that matters. You know what they say, today's news is tomorrow's history. We've just got to focus on getting Mokoto back now, too. But first things first…" he told them, rotating his aching shoulders.

"Strawberries and tea?" Mokoto asked hopefully, thinking George's plan was to head into the kitchen.

"We've got to get rid of the masses out there," he nodded towards the door and furrowed his brow.

"Be careful now," Grandpa Frank cautioned him. His only son looked like he was preparing for a confrontation and he didn't want him getting into any trouble.

George confidently strode over to the door and readied himself for a battle. He momentarily paused, took a deep breath, then opened the door slightly, slipped through and pulled it shut it behind him.

A long, furry microphone was immediately shoved in his face and flashes of light temporarily dazzled him.

He held his forearms up to shield his eyes, then yelled at the invasive group, "You've all got to leave. Now. You've no right to be here and if you don't go now I'm calling the police!"

The crowd jostled and the photos continued until a voice from the back piped up, "We've got every right to be here, sorry buddy."

"Yeh, we've paid our dues!" another voice protested.

"What dues?" George was genuinely puzzled.

"The dude down the corridor, in apartment 4F," one of the more relaxed photographers explained. "He's a journalist. He says we can remain here as a guest of his, and use his bathroom and kitchen, for a daily fee."

"Hey!" George yelled out in dismay, elbowing his way through the hordes of people and equipment before banging on the door of 4F.

A young, thin man in spectacles peeped his head out like a timid mouse.

"What do you think you're doing?" George howled at him. "Get these people out of here!"

"Sorry man," he stammered, running his hand through his greasy mop of mousey hair. "I've got rent to pay. I need cash."

"Well they're wasting their money!" George blurted out defiantly. "They're not gonna see anything!"

"Okay man," the resident murmured back dismissively. "I've got a piece due in this afternoon, I've gotta get back to my computer." Then he slammed the door in George's face, before briefly opening it again, popping his head out and asking the crowd, "Anyone need to use the bathroom now, before I settle back at my desk?"

"No!" came a chorus of replies, so he disappeared again.

George nudged, jabbed and squeezed his way back towards his sister's apartment before turning around to the persistent pack and declaring, "You'll never see him, and we'll never tell you anything, so enjoy your time crammed into this crowded hallway. You all stink!"

It was a frustrated attempt at showing his outrage at their invasion, but he immediately recognized that it sounded a bit pathetic.

He used his key to get back into the apartment and, once again, had to physically stop the masses from trying to ram their cameras in.

"They're not going anywhere," he reluctantly conceded defeat, as he shut them out with his back against the door. "We're not going to be able to get Mokoto out tonight."

# CHAPTER 14

Mia had just gone into the kitchen to wash some strawberries and make some tea when she let out an ear-piercing scream. There was a determined face at the window with a camera, sending a series of flashing lights into Mia's eyes. She jumped up to pull the curtains closed, then frantically rushed through the apartment closing all the others.

"They're everywhere!" she wailed to her mother on the phone, "Climbing up the outside walls like spiders!"

"Just don't leave the apartment, whatever you do," Lana warned her, "I don't want you being caught up in their madness."

Grandpa Frank had gone to shower and change into a fresh shirt, then he, George and Mia gathered to eat around the dining room table, under artificial light, while the sunlight that usually flooded the apartment was blocked to keep out the brazen intruders.

"I feel like a fugitive, in hiding," Mia complained.

"It feels like night time during the day," Mokoto agreed, as he feasted on handfuls of strawberries in the paddling pool and slurped his delicious tea.

"Well something has to be done!" Grandpa Frank rallied the troops. "You're our master planner," he looked at Mia, "try and think of something!"

Just then they were startled by a fierce banging on the door.

"Open up! Police!" a stern voice bellowed.

The family looked at each other in stunned silence.

Mokoto froze, with the juice from a mouthful of strawberries oozing from his lips. He didn't know what the police were, but he knew from the stern tone, and the family's reaction, that something serious was happening. He instinctively wanted to slope off and bury himself behind some coral, but there was nowhere to go and nowhere to hide

"What shall we do?" Mia whispered, without daring to move an inch.

"Ignore them!" George mouthed urgently.

"Open up!" a voice repeated, with rising insistence. They clearly weren't going away.

"Hide Mokoto in the bathroom!" Grandpa Frank suddenly wheezed at the others, so George and Mia shot up to go and grab him.

George gripped Mokoto under the arms, and Mia took the weight of his tail as they scrambled into the bathroom to lay Mokoto down in the tub.

"What's happening?" he breathed anxiously, his blue eyes wracked with fright, "Are they going to take me away?"

"We won't let them!" George reassured him, "Just stay in here and keep quiet."

"We know you're in there! Open the door now!" The fierce bangs matched the intensity of Mia's heartbeats and echoed through the small apartment.

George sidled up to the door and closed his eyes as he slowly opened it, as if he was expecting to be ambushed.

"Can I see some ID please?" he squeaked, just as a police badge flew towards his face, stopping right in front of his nose. "Okay," he yelped, as he looked at it cross-eyed. "Come in."

Two police officers marched into the apartment, accompanied by two academic looking men dressed in white coats, with pens poking out of their top pockets.

The cameras flashed furiously behind them before George shut the door on the intrusive world of chaos.

"Can I help you?" he inquired feebly, as his mind crawled with an infestation of thoughts about why they were there -each one like a hungry rat gnawing on his tired brain.

Did they know he was responsible for the missing

dolphins? Did they want Mokoto? Were they going to ask Mia about the stolen pool mattresses?

The male police officer glared at the empty paddling pool, while the female officer bore holes in George's eyes with a laser stare.

"We know what you've been up to," she scowled.

George gulped and Mia glanced at her grandfather nervously.

"Harbouring an unknown, exotic pet," the male officer added. "It's dangerous and you're going to have to surrender him."

"Exotic pet?" George looked baffled.

"The merman!" the female officer clarified, while she stood there with her hands behind her back, glowering at him as if he was a student who'd just got the worst test score in the class. "The game's up! We've all seen him on TV and we know you've been keeping him here. It's beginning to cause a public disturbance!"

"I might just interrupt if I may," one of the men in white coats spoke with soft intensity. "My colleague and I work for the government office of Marine Conservation." He twiddled with the lids of the pens in his top pocket and loudly swallowed his excess saliva. "We've been very interested in your story, and after an emergency meeting early this morning, we've decided that we should seize...I mean take custody...of the merman."

"It's in everyone's best interests," his slightly taller colleague chimed in, excitedly. "The scales can tell us which fish he's most closely related to, his respiratory system can offer us insights into how humans might one day spend more time under water. We want to know about the structure of his muscles, his circulatory system and cardio output. We want to test his senses and monitor his brain activity. We know from the fishmonger's story that he speaks English. We want to know how else he communicates. It's all quite thrilling."

The smaller scientist nodded gently, trying to restrain the true extent of his enthusiasm, which, in reality, made him want to leap up and thump the ceiling with joy. "We want to test his strength and resilience. We want to see if his tissue regenerates and we want to investigate the possibility of cloning, so that we can create more of the same and put them to good use."

Mia raised her hands up to her flushed cheeks in horror.

"Where's the creature now?" the male police officer held onto the sides of his belt and tapped his polished shoe.

No one dared answer. They didn't want to lie to the police, but they certainly didn't want to tell the truth either, so Grandpa Frank, George and Mia all looked down awkwardly at the floor.

The female police officer's eyes followed the trail of water from the paddling pool to the bathroom.

"Mind if I step in there?" she pointed to the bathroom door.

"No!" George screamed urgently.

The officer looked taken aback and sunk her face into her neck, displaying a fleshy pile of double chins.

"No, you don't mind?" the male officer asked.

"No, I mean no you can't!" George responded firmly.

"We just want to take a look at him," the taller scientist explained. "So we can decide how it would be best to safely transport him to our facility. Does he need regular exposure to water? Or can he withstand long periods of dryness?"

Again, the family looked down, hunching their shoulders and sneaking uncomfortable looks at each other.

"We're gonna go ahead and get a warrant from the court today to search this place," the male police officer crackled, with a wry smile.

"Call us when you're ready for the merman to be picked up," his colleague hissed, "otherwise we'll be here at eight o'clock tomorrow morning with a warrant to search and seize. We'll have transport to take him to his new home. Understand?" she smirked.

George nodded reluctantly.

"Meanwhile we're gonna keep two officers outside your door here, make sure you don't try to move him." She raised her eyebrows, as if to warn him not to try any funny business.

"Please understand," the smaller scientist tried to console them, "we'll take very good care of him. He's unique; completely one of a kind. You can trust us to keep him alive and well."

The family's unwanted visitors then headed towards the door and waited for George to open it. When they stepped back into the lights and cameras, they stood to pose for photos, lapping up their five minutes of fame.

"This can't happen!" Mia shrieked, as soon as they were out of earshot. "We can't let Mokoto go with them!"

"I'm not sure we're going to have much choice in this Mia," George mumbled sadly.

"Mia's right!" Grandpa Frank felt a fighting spirit soaring through his aged body. "We've got a duty to defend him. We have to get him back in the ocean!"

"Is everything okay now?" they heard Mokoto's gentle voice drift faintly from the bathroom.

Mia immediately ran to him and took his hand in hers.

"The people who run the country, the people who are in charge, they want to take you. But we're not going to let them, so you've got nothing to worry about. We're not going to allow it." She squeezed his hand tightly.

"Are you okay, Mia?" he looked at her solemn face with concern.

"I'm fine," she lied, trying to swallow away the painful lump in her throat as she struggled to hold back her tears.

"I think it's safer that he stays in here for now," George appeared next to her and started filling the bathtub with water, "in case we have any other surprise visitors."

# CHAPTER 15

Mia spent the rest of the morning in the bathroom, reading to Mokoto from a kids' encyclopaedia about how things are made. She described how electricity works and how buildings are constructed, how car engines operate and how airplanes fly up into the sky. She showed him pictures and recounted her own experiences. It was as much to distract herself from her rising anxiety as it was to enlighten her mer-friend.

Mokoto listened intently and asked lots of questions, before finally looking at Mia and saying, "You live in a wonderful world, full of so many great inventions. So why are so many legpeople mean and unhappy? In the Coral Kingdom we have nothing except what nature has given us, and we're all happy and kind to each other."

"I'm not sure," Mia replied truthfully. "But I do know there are lots of very kind, caring people too, who want to help others and be nice to everyone. I also know it's important for people to try and surround themselves with kind and happy people, or, sooner or later, they'll become mean and unhappy too. That's why I like spending time with my family. They're all kind and nice."

"I've got to get back to work now," George popped his head around the door. "Call me when your mom gets home, okay?"

"Okay," Mia tried to offer a convincing smile back, but her heart was too heavy. She felt as if it was a balloon being slowly filled with water, and as each hour counted down, it was closer to bursting.

"Mokoto," she pleaded, "help me come up with a plan, because I can't think of what we should do..."

"Mia!" Grandpa Frank called out to her from his brown, velvet armchair, "Get over here!"

Grandpa Frank, like the rest of the family, rarely watched television, but he, too, was trying to distract himself from the reality of their daunting situation. A local reporter was down at the harbour, bringing live, breaking news that the whale had returned to the same spot where it was lingering before, and was baffling scientists with its behaviour.

"As I speak," the reporter chatted in an upbeat way, waving her hands around in an animated style, "a group of marine biologists are on a boat heading out to the whale, and they're going to fit it with a tracking device to send out more information to them about where it travels to when it leaves the harbour area."

"And how will they do that?" the chirpy presenter in the newsroom asked.

"The transmitter will be attached to a dart, which will be placed just behind the whale's blowhole and embedded in its blubber. Scientists believe it's a painless procedure." The reporter's inane grin irked Grandpa Frank and he promptly switched off the TV.

"Oh no!" Mia gasped, "She might lead them back to the merpeople!"

"This has gone too far," Grandpa Frank grumbled, shaking his head.

Mia rushed back into the bathroom to tell Mokoto about Nui's return.

"She won't leave without me," Mokoto said with certainty. "She might be there for the rest of her life," he added, sadly.

"Don't say that!" Mia scolded him. "We're going to get you out of here! We just have to think hard about what we should do."

Mokoto and Mia then threw around a steady stream of suggestions, and dismissed them one by one, until Lana returned home from work.

There were two reporters waiting on the street, outside the apartment block, but they had no idea who Lana was, so she rushed past them without arousing suspicion. She was then astounded by just how many journalists were in the hallway on the fourth floor, outside her door. Things were surprisingly quiet, with only a general hum of low key conversations and the odd eruption of laughter. When it became clear that Lana was entering the merman's apartment, however, the whole floor erupted into a furore of lights, cameras and microphones, and she was hit with a barrage of questions.

"What's his name?"

"Why are you keeping him?"

"Where's his family?"

Lana kept her head down and didn't acknowledge them.

"Are you in love with him, lady?" asked a bolder journalist, looking for an even more sensational headline.

Lana swung around and glared at him.

"Hey! Just doing my job!" he shrugged his shoulders nonchalantly.

She pushed and elbowed her way past them and eventually made her way to two police officers standing guard outside her door. They refused to move, until she explained that she lived there and produced her key.

She burst inside with a desperate look of dismay.

"It's even worse than you described!" she called to Mia and Grandpa Frank.

Mia ran out of the bathroom and immediately began telling her mother about Nui.

"Why are the curtains closed?" Lana asked, and before Mia had a chance to explain, Lana went to open the curtains in the living room, only to reveal the face of a man with a long moustache and chin full of stubble pressed against the window.

"Ahhhhh!" she screamed out as she jumped back in horror.

"Wait!" he shouted through the glass. "I'm not a journalist or a reporter, I'm here to help you! But I can't get in the building!"

Once she'd regained her composure, Lana felt totally perplexed, so she couldn't resist edging back closer to him and asking, "How did you even get up here?"

"I brought a ladder around. Sorry!" he shouted back, occasionally peering at the street below with a look of dread. He was wearing a crumpled business shirt and had a thick, short, gold necklace around his neck.

"I can offer you a solution to everything. We need to talk! Can you just come down and let me in so I can get off this ladder?" he pleaded, as he looked down again and grimaced at the distance between himself and the pavement.

Lana then grabbed Grandpa Frank's walking stick and wedged it in the window rail, so that she could open the window only ever so slightly before it got jammed against the stick. Mia shuffled over to stand beside her.

"Why are you here?" Lana spoke through the tiny gap as the man balanced against the window ledge outside, with his feet on the top rung of the ladder.

"I've got a place where you can keep your merman!" he breathed, with an expectant look. "He'll have lots of space and it's right next to the sea!"

Mia was puzzled.

"Do you live in a mansion?" she asked.

"I'm the owner of the dolphinarium!" he explained.

Lana drew her head back and cringed with disgust.

"I've lost everything," he complained. A strong breeze swept his long moustache to the side, but the black hair on his head didn't move at all. It was gelled back into a low ponytail, with only a few stubborn, grey strands refusing to conform.

"And no one even seems to care that much," he added, not daring to take his hand off the window ledge to smooth his moustache back in place.

"I wonder why," Lana whispered sarcastically under her breath.

"They're all more interested in your merman," he grumbled. "I have to refund everyone who pre-bought tickets for today, and by the end of the month, with no dolphins, and no customers, I won't even be able to pay the mortgage on the dolphinarium. I can get more dolphins, but by the time I've trained them I'll have lost too much money already."

"What's this got to do with us?" Lana asked impatiently.

"I've got the space, you've got the attraction, together we

could make a lot of money! I'd be back in business! People would love seeing a real, live merman!"

"When are you going to learn?" she spat at him irritably. "Sea creatures aren't yours to steal, confine and display like flowers in a garden. They're intelligent beings that have their own lives, their own homes, their own families."

Mia lightly kicked her mother to stop. She was worried that her vocal opposition to this man's outlook might raise his suspicions.

"I'm sorry about your bad luck," Mia lied through the tiny gap. "But my teacher says that we should try and treat every ending as a new beginning. It was probably time to change your business anyway, because it wasn't likely to keep doing well. You see, more and more people are learning about how it's cruel to keep dolphins in captivity. Kids like me don't want to see dolphins in swimming pools. We want to see them enjoying their freedom in the open ocean, out in the wild, where they belong. We want to see them happy."

The owner of the dolphinarium tilted his head to the side and looked as if he might actually be thinking about what Mia was saying.

"If I was you," she continued, "I'd sell the dolphinarium and buy a big boat to take people out dolphin watching in the wild. I think that would be a great business!"

Lana and Mia both stared at him and he narrowed his eyes back at them thoughtfully.

"Is there no way you'll even consider putting the merman in my big pool?" the desperate man gave it one last try.

"No!" Lana barked back. "Now get off my ledge and don't come back! I've got enough on my plate at the moment without being shocked by strangers at my window! Goodbye!"

With that, she slammed the window shut and closed the curtains.

"The nerve of the man!" Lana cried out.

"Yes," Mia agreed, "but he's given me a wonderful idea..."

# CHAPTER 16

Mia called Uncle George. His boat had returned to the harbour and he was helping his last passenger onto the dock. The late afternoon sun hung low in the sky and bathed everything in warm orange shadows. It was one of his favourite times of the day, but his concern for Mokoto prevented him from fully appreciating it. He'd seen Nui out beyond the harbour walls but couldn't get too close as there was already a fluster of other vessels crowded around her. He wondered forlornly about how long she'd have to wait there and if she'd ever see Mokoto again.

"Mum's home. We need a family meeting. Can you come over now?" Mia sounded a lot more cheery than when George had left her.

"I'm on my way!" he assured her, as helpful as ever.

When George pulled up outside the apartment block, there was only one reporter waiting outside. A woman with a shock of red hair tumbling down her shoulders. She rushed over to George with her camera as soon as he got out of his pick-up truck.

"Listen," she said, her freckled face looking serious and businesslike, "we want your story. And we're willing to pay big. Can we agree to meet in the apartment so I can film the merman and interview the family?"

"We're not interested," George told her firmly, marching towards the entrance.

"You're being foolish!" the woman shouted after him. "This could make you rich, it's easy money, but you're making a stand just for the sake of a stupid fish man!"

"Now you listen to me," George turned around and looked her straight in the eye. "Some things mean more than money."

The reporter rolled her eyes.

George then repeated his father's words, "There's something called integrity that runs in our family. Look it up."

By this time, a few of the journalists in the hallway had left, but there were still enough to make passing through seem like a tricky obstacle course. George shouldered his way onwards and stepped over various equipment before coming face to face with the police officers outside the apartment door.

"Not long to go now," one of the officers remarked to the other, clearly intending for George to hear.

"I can't wait for them to take him out so we can all see him," the other smirked back.

"Excuse me," George stated, sternly.

The officers chuckled to each other as they slowly stepped aside so he could let himself in with his key. He didn't want to knock at the door and have any of his family be confronted by the media madness outside when they opened it.

"Meeting. In the bathroom. Now." Lana told her brother as soon as she saw his sun-kissed face.

George picked up a kitchen chair and took it through to the bathroom for Grandpa Frank to sit on, but when he looked back at his father and saw him slowly heading towards his bedroom, not the bathroom, he called out after him.

"Hey, Dad, where you going?"

"Come with me for a moment please, son," he whispered. "I need you to help me with something."

George followed Grandpa Frank into the small room. His single bed took up most of the space and a framed photo of his late wife, George's mother, who he said goodnight to every evening, took pride of place on his bedside table.

Grandpa Frank eased himself down onto the edge of the bed and placed both hands on his walking stick.

"Can you open the wardrobe please?"

George pulled open the double doors of the dark, wooden wardrobe to reveal Grandpa Frank's neat row of checked shirts and carefully folded jumpers. He didn't have much, but what he did have, he took good care of.

"On the shelf at the top," he directed George, "there's an old chest from when I was a boy. "Can you get it down for me?"

George reached up and grabbed a large, antique, wooden trunk with brass clasps. He quickly realised how heavy it was when he strained as he pulled it into his arms.

"It was given to me by my father, your Grandpa Haku, when I was twelve years old," he explained. "It's my box of memories. There are old letters from your mother in there and photos of my youth."

George smiled at his father affectionately as he held his history in his arms.

"Can you carry it into the bathroom for me, please George?"

"No problem," George agreed, as they ambled their way over to the others.

Lana and Mia were sitting on the mat next to Mokoto. George put the wooden chest down just in front of Grandpa Frank's seat, and then sat down on the toilet seat.

"Mokoto's must get out of here. Tonight." Mia told the others, as she scanned her family's attentive faces.

"We're not going to get past the police at the door," George shook his head at Mia hopelessly.

"Exactly!" Mia responded. "So we're going to use your ladder to get out through the living room window!"

There was a stunned silence as they all imagined the potential scenario.

"We won't be able to carry Mokoto down the ladder," Lana complained, imagining what a disaster that would turn into.

"I know," Mia replied confidently, eager to prove that she'd fully thought this through. "We'll lower him down in the tarpaulin."

"How?" Lana asked, keen to try and visualise it in her mind.

"The tarpaulin that we used to save the dolphins has holes along the two long sides that are strengthened with metal hoops. We need to cut the material shorter, so it's just a bit longer than Mokoto's body. About the same length as Uncle George, then half as much again, I'd say. Then we need to lay Mokoto on the tarpaulin, so the holes are either side of him, and loop some of the strong rope from Uncle George's boat through the holes. I'd say we need four pieces of long rope that are at least twice the length of the distance between our apartment window and the ground. One to loop together the holes near his head, another one for the tail, and two at equal intervals along his body."

"I haven't got that much rope in my boat," George told her, "but I can go to the store if I leave soon."

"And the reporters outside the building? What about them?" Grandpa Frank asked.

"There was only one there when I just came in," George reported.

"Hopefully there won't be any there when it gets dark. But even if there are, surely they have to sleep at some stage?" Mia reasoned.

Grandpa Frank nodded his head enthusiastically, "I knew you'd come up with something!" he winked at his grand-daughter. "I think it's a good plan, we should do it!"

"We'll have to keep our ear to the door and try to guess when the reporters in the hallway have gone to sleep. And we'll have to keep checking out of the window to see when the coast is clear on the street," Mia explained. "When everything's quiet, we'll call you, Uncle George. You'll need to bring the ladder, the tarpaulin and the rope."

"It could be really late by the time it's safe to leave though," Lana looked concerned. "It might not leave enough time for George to get back to work in the morning."

"That's not a problem," George reassured them all. "I only had a handful of customers booked for tomorrow morning, so I already rescheduled them onto the afternoon trip because it wasn't cost effective."

"Perfect!" Mia cried out.

"I don't know," Lana's face was wracked with concern as she gazed at a rubber duck bobbing along in Mokoto's bathtub.

"What if the reporters are doing shift work and get replaced with more reporters who'll stay up all night? And I doubt the police will go to sleep. They'll hear us. It all sounds too risky."

"What choice do we have though, Lanie?" George reasoned with her. "If we do nothing, they're going to take him in the morning."

"Please try!" Mokoto pleaded with her from the tub. "I have to get back to my family!"

There was a momentary pause when all eyes were on Lana.

"Okay," she finally looked up at her family. "Let's do it."

"I'll go and buy some rope and wait for your call..." George began to stand up.

"Wait, sit down son," Grandpa Frank's eyebrows gestured towards the toilet seat, so George promptly took his place there again.

"There's something I need to tell you." He tightened his grip on his walking stick and looked down at his slippers as he thought about where to begin.

"Our family has a long history of being connected to the ocean. It's in our blood. It's where we find happiness."

George nodded and thought about how much he loved being out on his boat in the sunshine, with mists of fresh sea spray spattering his bronzed cheeks. Mia reflected on how thrilling it was to ride her surfboard; the addictive rush she felt when she caught a wave and carved her way along watery hills of turquoise, with the sun on her skin and the wind in her hair. Lana's mind took her to the beach, her favourite place, where she loved seeing the sunrise greet the shore and blanket the gently rippling water in shimmering shades of red and yellow.

"Our ancestors have always lived and worked in and around the ocean." Grandpa Frank looked at each of them with his sparkling green eyes. "My great-great-grandfather was a fisherman and he had a close group of friends who he fished with for many years. They'd spend days and nights on their boat; the sea was their home."

He stopped briefly to clear his throat, then continued,

"They travelled for hundreds of miles, searching for new waters to cast their nets. Then one day, they came across a perfect little island, shining alone in the afternoon sun. There seemed to be nothing on it, except a few palm trees, so they threw their anchor in and waded onto the sand to eat their lunch. That's when they saw them. A group of merpeople, relaxing in the clear water, further up the beach. There were three mermaids and one merman."

The family all stared at him, enthralled by his story.

"Now these fishermen had heard seafaring tales of mermaids and mermen, but they never thought they were true, until that moment. They went over to the group with big smiles on their faces and showed that they were friendly. They communicated through hand gestures and began to make the merpeople laugh. Grandpa Kai had quite the sense of humour apparently."

"Runs in the family!" George beamed.

"Kai?" Mokoto piped up, intrigued by the name.

"Yes," Grandpa Frank confirmed. "Kai Kalani."

Mokoto's jaw dropped. "Kai Kalani was your ancestor?" He felt a wondrous pulse of enlightenment surge though his body as he realised that his friends were related to this legendary figure. No wonder they were so kind.

"Yes," Grandpa Frank answered, "We're all Kalanis. I'm Frank Kalani."

"And I'm Mia Kalani," Mia smiled, then pointed at her mother and uncle, "Lana Kalani and George Kalani!"

"Kai Kalani had the Kalani green eyes and a relaxed, happy outlook on life that made everyone warm to him. He was also dependable and practical," Grandpa Frank carried on, "the merpeople loved him."

Lana looked at her brother affectionately and grinned.

"Now, the island was far away, but Grandpa Kai and his group of fishermen tried to return every few months or so, to meet up with their new friends. They played games with them, shared food with them and taught them how to speak English."

"That's how you know!" Mia beamed at Mokoto.

"And they found out that they loved strawberries and tea."

"That's how you knew!" Lana gently shook her head at her father in shock and disbelief.

"The merpeople tried to teach the fishermen their own language too, but they found it quite hard to get their tongues around all the bubble sounds."

"It's easy, there's nothing to it!" Mokoto cried out in Mermish, through a series of burbled, churning, gurgling, bubbly sounds that made the family gasp and giggle.

"The merpeople introduced the fishermen to the rest of their community, who swam over to the island to spend time with Grandpa Kai and the others. They told them about their enchanted life beneath the waves, in a place called The Coral Kingdom."

"Home," Mokoto reminisced with a sigh.

"Now Grandpa Kai and his friends knew that if they told anyone about the merpeople, that would be the end of them."

"That was smart," Mia muttered, thinking about all the trouble Mokoto's presence had caused.

"But Grandpa Kai didn't want the secret to be lost forever." Grandpa Frank stopped to reach for the wooden chest at his feet. The old brass clasps clicked as he slowly opened them, and the lid creaked as he pushed it up.

George, Lana and Mia leaned forward to see what was inside, then Grandpa Frank pulled out a sphere shaped object, wrapped in blue, velvet cloth.

"Grandpa Kai became very old, and on one of his last visits the merpeople gave him this, in recognition of the many happy times they'd spent together." Grandpa Frank pulled away the velvet from the object on his knee and revealed the largest white pearl they'd ever seen. It was about the size of a tennis ball and had a flawless, bright finish that radiated around the room.

"Wow! It's so beautiful!" Lana gasped

"Stunning!" George agreed, while Mia's eyes fixated on it in fascination.

Mokoto was spellbound and thought about the dip in the

rock where it would have originally been displayed, at the top of the archway entrance to The Coral Kingdom.

"This has been handed down through generations of Kalanis," Grandpa Frank told them. "And we've passed on the story of the merpeople."

Lana, George and Mia reached to stroke the smooth, hard exterior of the perfect pearl.

"My grandfather had his doubts about the whole thing, and my father thought it was probably just a family fairy tale. But I knew the truth. You can trust the word of a Kalani."

Grandpa Frank's family smiled at him in a shared moment of pride and unity.

"But I want you to have it back now," Grandpa Frank looked earnestly at Mokoto. "Take it back with you. Tell the merpeople that it's a symbol of our friendship and goodwill. Tell them that there are kind legpeople here who care about them and treasure their magical existence. But warn them that our land is no place for a merman or a mermaid. They shouldn't try to come here again."

# CHAPTER 17

That evening, Lana and Mia used buckets to empty the paddling pool of water, then dragged it through to the kitchen, to make a space in the living room.

The surveillance checks started at nine o'clock. Mia pressed her ear against the front door to listen for sounds from the reporters and police. They were still chatting and she could hear occasional bursts of laughter. She shook her head with frustration and wondered how long it would take for them to start feeling tired.

Lana, meanwhile, was peering out from the smallest possible gap in the curtains. The woman who'd ran up to George earlier was still there, sitting in her own portable chair, waiting in hope that the family might try to venture out of the apartment building with the merman.

Time was ticking down and they paced anxiously around the apartment, like caged tigers, desperate for the earliest opportunity to break out of their confinement.

Grandpa Frank was staying up late to watch the great escape. He felt sad that his aging limbs weren't going to allow him to climb down the ladder and go with them. He couldn't deny the air of excitement and anticipation that filled the air, however, as his trustworthy family waited for the golden moment to carry out their ambitious plan.

On Lana's seventh check, she squealed quietly with delight when she saw a car pull up and watched the red-headed, waiting reporter shove her folded up, portable chair into the back seat before climbing in herself. The car then sped off into the darkness and the street was gloriously empty and quiet.

"How's it sounding out there?" she asked her daughter, as

Mia listened to persistent shuffling and murmurs.

"No change," she announced, with noticeable annoyance. "Don't these people ever sleep?"

Grandpa Frank was sitting in his armchair with the pearl on his knee, polishing it with the velvet fabric and trying to imagine it being back in its rightful home.

"You might just have to cut your losses and go for it," he advised his granddaughter. "At least it's clear outside."

"No Grandpa," Mia answered him decisively, "we have to wait for the best moment, or we risk ruining everything."

At midnight, that moment finally came. "I can't hear anything!" she whispered, flapping her hand excitedly while her ear was still pressed against the door.

"Keep listening!" Lana breathed back quietly. "We have to be sure!"

Mia continued to tune in attentively, until she felt confident that it was time to call George.

"Come now!" she told him on the phone. "The coast is clear and everything's quiet!"

The ladder, ropes, and two boxes of strawberries that he'd decided to buy, were ready and waiting in George's pick-up truck. He'd also cut the tarpaulin to size and stuffed it in a lightweight backpack, so it was easier to carry. As soon as he got the go-ahead, he raced away from his apartment with the speed and efficiency of a firefighter responding to an emergency call-out. He hurried over to his sister's home and was outside her apartment block within fifteen minutes.

When Lana saw her brother's truck pull up, her heart lurched. "This is it!" she announced nervously, placing one hand on her galloping heart in a useless attempt to rein it into a steady canter.

She and Mia watched through the curtain while George took the ladder out of the truck, rested it outside the wall of the apartment building, and began to extend it upwards to his sister's window. He then took four pieces of rope and wrapped each of them over his left shoulder and under his right arm, and back again, until they were safely fixed across his broad body. Finally, he took the backpack full of tarpaulin, flung it over his right shoulder and began to scale the ladder.

As he approached the fourth floor, Lana slowly and cautiously slid open the living room window, trying to minimize any noise. The warm night air flooded in as George pushed his body through and lifted his legs over the ledge, into the apartment.

Mia immediately reached for the backpack to grab the tarpaulin, and started to unfold it in the space where the paddling pool used to be. Lana helped to stretch out the sides, while George quickly unravelled the rope from his body.

"Let's get him!" Lana whispered, when the tarpaulin was fully laid out straight and the rope was in four piles beside it.

They all tiptoed over to the bathroom, mindful that a rush of heavy, plodding footsteps might vibrate into the hallway and wake their sleeping predators.

"It's time to go!" Mia breathed urgently to Mokoto, who sat bolt upright in the bathtub and took a deep breath to prepare himself.

George gripped him under his arms, in his usual way, Lana supported the top of his tail, while Mia lifted the end.

They silently shuffled out with him. George took the lead, walking backwards into the living room and constantly turning his head around to make sure they weren't going to bang into anything.

They laid him down in the middle of the tarpaulin then swiftly grabbed the long ropes and began to thread them through the holes.

By this time, Grandpa Frank had hobbled over to the tarpaulin. He held his back as he bent down to carefully place the pearl into the water creased palms of Mokoto's large hands. Then, in a moment that would linger for eternity in both of their hearts, Grandpa Frank's old, green eyes became locked in a gaze with Mokoto's blues, and they soaked in the energy of a centuries-old connection between them. It was an unspoken goodbye that spoke more than words ever could.

"Mum," Mia's whisper broke the silence, "you take the head rope. Uncle George, you take the two middle ropes. I'll take the tail rope."

Grandpa Frank stepped back as they each pulled the ends of their ropes together, and knotted them in the middle, so that the tarpaulin closed above Mokoto and his body was enveloped in the blue material.

Mia then hurried over to the living room window next to the one George had come in through and slowly opened it, without making a sound. She knew that they would risk knocking over the ladder if they lowered Mokoto out of the first window.

"Right, keep hold of the ropes and lift him to the window. We have to push him through sideways and make sure that his body's bent, so it fits," George directed, in hushed tones.

So they heaved Mokoto over and pushed him through the window frame, until the midpoint of his tarpaulin-covered body was poking outside, resting on the ledge, while his head and the rest of his tail were still inside.

"Okay, let's push him out and lower him." George muttered imperatively. "Hold on tight to the base of the ropes and only release them very slowly, as I say so." His heart was beating so furiously, he wondered if the thunderous echoes themselves might wake the people in the hallway.

Mokoto unintentionally let out a little yelp as they nudged him out, scared that he might plummet to the ground. It was a relief when he finally felt his legpeople friends tugging back to catch his weight.

The family slowly but surely lowered the ropes, but Lana and Mia soon realised that the friction was burning their soft hands.

Suddenly, Mokoto felt his body beginning to slide headfirst out of the open end of the tarpaulin. He instinctively thrust his right hand up through the middle portion of material to grab one of the ropes, while still clutching the precious pearl with the left.

"Lana!" George whispered urgently, "Pull your rope up

more! You have to release it at the same pace as us!"

"Sorry!" Lana mouthed back, as she began to hoist it back up to the same length as the others. Her hands were feeling painfully raw and it had affected her focus.

Mokoto's upper body jerked upwards again and he tried to wriggle his way back into his previous position, so his head wasn't so close to the opening.

"Keep still!" Mia warned him quietly. "You're making the ropes swing!"

"Slowly, slowly," George gently guided them, "a little lower on the tail. There we go, that's perfect, keep going, easy does it."

It was a lot more difficult and dangerous than Mia had imagined, so she breathed out a heavy sigh of relief when Mokoto's body finally touched down on a small verge of grass, behind a bush outside the apartment building.

"Go, go, go!" George told them, and they all sped back to the other window on their tiptoes.

Mia was first to clamber through and edge her way down the rungs. She'd never been so high up on a ladder before and it felt worryingly unsteady.

Grandpa Frank had joined Lana and George at the window, to watch his granddaughter's descent.

"Try to keep steady!" he wheezed, "Don't try and go too fast!"

"And don't look down!" George whispered, "Trust your footing!"

Mia let out quiet whimpers with every trembling step she took. The ladder didn't feel safe and seemed to shake with every small movement she made. When she eventually reached the ground, her legs were like jelly and she had to urgently will the strength back into them.

Lana was next to climb out, determined to glide down as quickly as possible. Thankfully, the benefits of her teenage, summer window cleaning job many years previously paid off beautifully, and she eased herself down like a professional.

George came last of all. His practice the night before, racing up and down the ladder saving the dolphins, ensured that he was as sure-footed as a mountain goat, and he quietly flew down with ease.

"You okay?" George asked Mia softly.

"Fine. Let's get Mokoto in the tray," Mia was single-minded and didn't want to waste time with small talk.

They ran over to Mokoto, on the ground, and George counted to three before they lifted him up and scrambled over to the truck.

The end of Mokoto's tail had started to protrude through the end of the tarpaulin, however, and as they squeezed their way along the bush and past the ladder, to get to the pavement, the tip of one of his huge flukes hooked onto a rung. They all felt the weight of the tug and froze with shock as they watched the top of the ladder pull away from the wall.

There was a split second when they thought it might topple over. Instead, it rebounded back against the wall, making a clattering sound and causing a few lights to be turned on in the apartment building.

"Oh no!' Lana shrieked, "Run!"

# CHAPTER 18

George had intended to collapse the ladder and take it with them, but he had no choice now. He had to leave it.

The loud noise had reverberated around their bodies like fireworks, charging him, Lana and Mia with sparks of unexpected strength. They shot over to the truck and flung Mokoto into the tray as fast as they could. Mokoto cried out in pain as his nose slammed into the hard metal, but they didn't have time to stop.

George and Lana bounded into the front seats, slamming the doors shut behind them. Mia jumped into the tray with Mokoto.

George started the engine and pressed the pedal so his foot hit the floor, sending them jolting forward and careering down the street with an urgent screech.

By this time, the press reporters and the police officers were flooding out of the entrance to the apartment building like a torrent of unstoppable water bursting through a pipe.

"They're coming!" Lana cried, twisting her body to see the mad rush of people and cameras jumping into vehicles behind them.

Grandpa Frank was watching from the apartment window and clutched his chest in terror. "Go on my Kalanis, you can do this!" he rasped.

As George skidded around the corner and accelerated into the quiet main road, the truck powered its way through a series of green lights until their pursuers were no longer in sight.

Mia was bumping around in the tray, frantically trying to undo the knots in the four ropes that held the tarpaulin together around Mokoto's body. As she untied the first and saw his face, his eyes were closed tight with fright, with his long, white lashes pressing into his tense cheeks.

"Are you okay Mokoto?" Mia shouted, her tender tone being lost in the rush of wind that swept around them with the speed of the vehicle.

"They're going to get us, aren't they?" Mokoto shouted back, without opening his eyes.

"I don't know," Mia screamed back truthfully, "but we're trying our best."

She furiously scrambled to untie the other knots. Her body was continuously being slammed about, but she knew it would be easier for them to lift Mokoto out of the truck without all the tarpaulin and ropes caught up around him. When she pulled apart the blue sheet, she saw him desperately clutching the pearl with both hands.

Mia grabbed hold of the side of the tray and pulled herself up. Her long curls flew out behind her in the raging wind. She could hear the police siren, but she couldn't see their car, and her uncle seemed to be putting a reassuring distance between themselves and the pack behind them.

She lay down beside Mokoto and linked her arm through his.

"Open your eyes," she yelled into the wind. "Open them!"

Mokoto slowly managed to prize apart his eyelids and peer up into the night sky.

"Look at the stars!" she screamed, as they soared along the road.

"I'm looking!" Mokoto shouted back, with the twinkling lights reflecting in his blue eyes.

"Whatever happens," Mia told him urgently, "just know that we'll always be looking up into the same night sky. Seeing the same shining patterns in the darkness. And know that Grandpa Frank, Uncle George, Mum and I will always be here, below these stars. Thinking of you. And always wishing the best for you. Wherever you are."

For a brief moment, they were in the quiet eye of the raging storm around them, letting the depth of Mia's words seep into their hearts.

"Same," Mokoto called out, and turned his face to look at her.

"Your nose is red!" she cried out.

"It hurts," he complained.

"So do my hands," she yelled back, lifting her right hand to show her red, raw palm.

All of a sudden, the truck lurched forward even faster and they felt it sway slightly to the side as George battled to keep control.

Mia unlinked her arm and tried to lift herself up onto her elbows as the truck shook and rattled. She could only just see above the top of the tray, but the police car was there, further down the street, followed by a mass of preying vehicles. Reporters were leaning out of their car windows, filming the chase, hoping to capture the dramatic moment that George's truck was apprehended.

"They're catching up with us!" Lana screeched at George in the front, wildly swinging her head back and forth as she looked at the mob behind and the road ahead.

George was clenching the steering wheel so tightly, his knuckles had turned white. As he swung right, into the road that led to the harbour, his muscles tightened and his face tensed with panic. The back wheels of the truck had skidded sideways and he wrestled to swerve them back on course.

Lana was screaming and holding onto the dashboard, while Mokoto and Mia, in the tray, had been knocked to one side and were yelling out in fear.

"We're not going to make it!" Lana shrieked, "They're getting too close!"

"Hold on tight!" George yelled back, through his rapid breathing, as he abruptly veered the truck left again.

Mokoto and Mia desperately pressed their hands against the sides of the tray to steady themselves and the tangy, acidic smell of burned, rubber tires rose up around them.

"Faster!" Lana shouted.

They hurtled onwards, with George skilfully navigating the harbour roads as the truck leaped, lurched and screeched towards its destination.

Then, as they raced towards the entrance to the harbour car park, they both howled in fright when they realised that the security barrier was down, blocking their path. George furiously hit the brake as hard as he could, but it was too late, and they barrelled towards the yellow and black striped metal strip.

They braced themselves for what seemed like an inevitable impact, when the truck finally shook to a standstill, just a hair width away from the obstacle in its path. Lana and George jolted back and fought to catch their breath.

The security guard jumped out of the seat in his small office next to the barrier when he heard the alarming screech of brakes, and darted over to the culprit.

George put his window down and saw the guard's name pinned to his blue shirt. "It's an emergency, Sanjeev," he pleaded, "I've got to get to my boat right away."

Sanjeev the guard shone his torch into the truck. It was clearly a getaway vehicle and he was determined to find out what was going on.

"What's in the tray?" Sanjeev snarled, feeling sure that they were hiding something.

"My daughter!" Lana muttered breathlessly, as she frantically kept looking behind for any sign of their pursuers.

George shook his head in deepening despair as the guard walked around to investigate the cargo tray.

They'd been caught. The game was up.

He looked at his sister hopelessly. "The barrier's never down in the day, when I'm here," he muttered sadly.

The guard directed his torchlight into Mokoto and Mia's faces, blinding them into the heart-racing seriousness of the moment. They raised their hands to shield their eyes, before he redirected his focus to illuminate Mokoto's shimmering tail. As he scanned the incredible length of him, he stood aghast, with his mouth open wide, and was momentarily captivated by the endless, glittering scales. He'd seen this merman in the news, but to witness him in real life was more mesmerising than he ever could have imagined.

Sanjeev shot back to George in the front seat, just as Lana saw the swarm of chasing cars turn the corner at the end of the road. They were almost behind the truck now, fervently steaming down the street in hot pursuit, ready to pounce on their stagnant prey. Her face fell into her hands and she held her head in anguish.

They were trapped.

"Please Sanjeev!" George begged, "We have to take him back!"

Sanjeev glared back at him.

"Please!" George implored, as he looked him in the eye.

Sanjay's face suddenly softened. "Sea creatures belong in the sea," he declared, in a friendlier tone. "Live and let live, that's what I say," and he swiftly opened the barrier with a simple click of his remote control.

"Thank you!" George and Lana both sang out in unison, thrilled by their unexpected reprieve, as George once again pressed the accelerator and sped into the car park.

"Good luck," Sanjeev called out to them in the warm night air, as he watched the truck charge ahead. He then closed the barrier and stepped back into his office, even though he could see the ambush of pursuing vehicles approaching the entrance.

George swerved into a parking space next to the jetty and the truck jerked back as they sprang to a halt. They threw open their doors and leaped out to grab Mokoto.

"They're at the barrier!" Lana looked at the entrance, but Sanjeev was taking a deliberately long time to come out of his office and let the ill-intentioned throng of cars in.

George grabbed Mokoto under the arms as Mia bounded out of the tray. "Get hold of his tail," he shouted to his niece. "Lana, get the boxes!"

Lana held the two big boxes of strawberries between her

hands and her chin and they all raced off down the jetty, towards the boat, with the salty sea breeze rushing past their faces.

"The barrier's open!" Mia yelled out, looking behind her. "They're coming in!"

"Don't look back!" George warned her, "Just keep going!"

Mokoto's startled eyes darted back and forth between Mia and the advancing trail of headlights that were hurtling into the car park. He'd never felt so afraid. His long, yellow hair brushed the creaking pathway of wooden planks below and each thud of the family's frantic footsteps vibrated through his anxious body.

George's cheeks were puffed out and his red face strained as he charged onward with the strength of a bull, while Mia and Lana raced to keep up the pace. As they pounded past all the other vessels moored in the harbour, George's boat seemed agonisingly far away.

Just as it eventually came within sight, the family heard a mass of thunderous footsteps descending onto the pathway behind them. They shook as the stomping sound reverberated along the wooden track and growled at their feet like a hungry pack of wolves. The mob drew closer in a terrifying haze of furious stampeding, heavy breathing and urgent shouting.

As they reached the boat, George yelled at Lana, "Jump on!" Lana looked at the distance of water and wasn't sure if she could make it, but she took one step back and lunged herself forward, stumbling as her feet landed in the vessel.

"Pull that board out!" he frantically shouted at his sister, as she slammed down the boxes she was holding and reached for the long plank that was resting on one of the padded benches. She held it up and flung it down so that it bridged the boat to the land. George stepped onto it and hauled Mokoto onboard, but as Mokoto's body slumped down onto the deck, his tail flew up out of Mia's grip, and when it came crashing down again, it knocked the board into the sea before Mia had a chance to set foot on it.

"Jump!" her mother shrieked at her.

"No! Don't!" George shouted back, "Mia, untie the mooring rope while I start the engine!" George pointed to a small metal bollard protruding from the jetty and Mia began to quickly unravel the cord that secured the boat in its position.

After a couple of false starts, George fired up the engine, then Mia looked over and caught sight of her mother's eyes widen in terror. She quickly turned to see what she was staring at and found the police sprinting towards her, closely followed by a baying crowd of reporters, brandishing cameras and microphones.

"Quick Mia!" Lana screamed hysterically, leaning forward and reaching out for her daughter.

"Stop!" shouted the police officer, just as Mia unhooked the last piece of rope with her trembling hands. He then propelled himself forward and swiped his hand to grab hold of her arm.

"Mia!" Mokoto shrieked helplessly from the deck, while Lana let out a pained howl as she watched her daughter about to be wrenched into the hands of their determined pursuers.

Mia swung her arm back to avoid the officer's lunge, then threw herself towards the boat, with her long legs flying through the air, easily scaling the distance. The police officer landed flat on his face with a heavy thud.

Lana drew her daughter into her open arms as the boat pulled away, and the officer thumped the jetty in frustration as he watched them tear out of the harbour towards the open ocean.

They'd made it.

# CHAPTER 19

The jetty erupted into a frenzied, dazzling display of camera flashes that faded into the distance as the boat bounced across the ocean waves.

"Whoo-hoo!" George cheered, throwing his fist into the air as he embraced the exhilarating rush of welcome sea air that swept across his body.

He was elated that it had all worked out. There was a split second during their escape, when he was waiting for Lana to get the board out of the boat, that he considered dropping Mokoto into the water, so he could swim off on his own. Even in his state of panic, however, a sharp instinct told him that they needed to stick together and he felt a weight of responsibility towards his new mer-friend. He knew Mokoto would be tired, so facing the long journey alone would be too unsafe, and he didn't want to waste valuable time trying to find him again in the sea to put him back in the boat. He took a risk, but it had paid off to perfection.

Lana and Mia kneeled down to hug Mokoto. "We did it!" they sang out jubilantly.

"I really didn't think we would," Mokoto was still trying to calm himself, shaking his head in disbelief.

They then bounded over to George, at the wheel, and squeezed him tightly as he put one strong arm around them both and held them close. They stood together, wrapped in a comforting blanket of euphoria and relief, as George navigated a course away from their troubles in his trusted boat: The Pride of Kalani.

Soon after, he veered right and the loud whir of the engine subsided as it gradually slowed down to a low hum.

"What are you doing?" Lana asked, confused by their loss of speed.

"Nui!" Mia smiled, knowingly.

Just then a powerful surge of water burst into the air beside them and an enormous tail flipped out of the water.

The boat was now free floating and George dashed back to Mokoto, on the deck, to lift him onto one of the padded benches that bordered the sides of the boat, so he could see his old friend.

"Nui!" Mokoto's moonlit face was bathed in delight as he watched her enormous body glide beside them.

"Mokoto! You're finally here!" Nui boomed back in low, pulsed calls, as she gently nudged the starboard side.

"Can you lift me into the water please?" Mokoto looked at George pleadingly. He was desperate to feel the salt water on his skin again, to experience the liquid silk glide across his body, and to join his friend to celebrate their reunion.

"Sure!" George agreed.

Lana and Mia were back by George's side, so he carefully took the beautiful pearl out of Mokoto's protective grip and placed it inside a lifebuoy, beside the boxes of strawberries, before the three of them hoisted his body up and flipped him into the water.

Mokoto dived down as deeply as he could in one push, feeling the pleasurable pressure of the ocean against his tail, then soared back up under Nui's chin, playfully circling her flat head with happiness.

Nui was consumed with delight and stuck her tail up high into the air, before wildly swinging it around and slapping it down onto the water's surface, creating a giant splash and sending thunderous ripples through the water. It was a wonderfully contagious expression of joy that spread to the family's faces as they threw their arms around and cheered at the performance.

Mia squealed with delight and clapped her hands as she watched the heart-warming display, marvelling at how such a colossal creature could pull off such impressive stunts so effortlessly.

Nui's gigantic body continued to curve out of the water

and her tail rose up in a repeat show, while Mokoto's silver, blue and turquoise scales burst out of the depths beside her and wildly flailed around with excitement, showering the family with sea spray. His body then popped up to showcase his beaming smile, before he plunged back down, spinning his tail behind him.

It was glorious to see him back where he belonged, so full of life and vitality, releasing his energy in acrobatic movements that had been frustratingly denied to him over the past few days.

The two friends glided past each other, over and under each other, and continued their joyful aquatic dance in front of their enchanted audience.

They were so caught up in the moment, Mia almost forgot about the transmitter. "Uncle George!" she yelled out. The marine biologists put a tracker on Nui, Grandpa Frank and I saw it on the news!"

"Are you sure?" George asked.

"Yes, they said it was attached to a dart and they were putting it in her blubber!"

"Okay," George gathered his thoughts. "Hey, Mokoto!" he yelled out, as the happy merman's head emerged once more. "Tell Nui to get as close to the side of the boat as she can! I need to pull the tracker out!"

Mokoto dutifully dived back down and passed the message to Nui. Before they knew it, she'd edged the entire length of her immense body alongside the boat, and was floating submissively, like a patient waiting to be attended to by a doctor.

George leaned over as far as he could, but he still couldn't reach behind the whale's blowhole, where he knew they'd have tried to imbed the dart.

"Tell her to keep still!" George shouted over to Mokoto again, who was floating beside her. "I'll have to climb on her back!"

George swiftly removed his shirt, stood on the edge of the boat, and placed his foot onto the grey, mottled body of the enormous mammal. He took a few seconds to find his balance, as if he was on a surfboard, before crouching down and deftly slipping into a sitting position, with his legs straddled either side of Nui's giant back. He gently shifted his way forward and began to scan his hand around her soft blubber, below her blow hole. At first, he couldn't feel anything, but then he caught his hand on the protrusion and quickly yanked it out at an angle that wouldn't risk tearing her blubber.

"Got it!" he cried out, brandishing it in the air above his head, like a cowboy swinging a rope.

"What should we do with it?" Lana yelled out.

"I know!" Mokoto called, his gentle voice drifting from behind his friend's flipper. He reached over to George, who slid it down Nui's body towards him.

"Careful, it's sharp!" George warned him, but Mokoto caught it safely and clutched it in his hands.

Mokoto began making the familiar squawking and cooing sounds to summon any surrounding seagulls. Sure enough, within a minute, a small flock of them had reliably fluttered their way over and were suspended in the air around him.

"Friends!" he squawked to the feathered group. "I need your help! Please take this and fly back to the land with it. Try and find a shop, in the middle of the town, with a red and white canopy outside the front. It's at the top of a hill and has a picture of a fish on the front door. When you see it, please swoop down and gently drop this outside the back door."

"Okay!" the seagulls squawked back obligingly, before one of them swiped the transmitter from his hand and the flock flew away together to complete their task.

"What did you tell them?" Mia asked, excitedly.

"Let's just say, the fishmonger might get an unwelcome surprise tomorrow," Mokoto smiled back, before dipping back under the water.

"We better get going," Lana urged everyone. "We don't know if they'll call the coast guard. We should get out of here."

George eased himself onto his feet and carefully stepped onto the side of the boat before jumping back onto the deck. Nui immediately expressed her gratitude through a series of happy leaping and tail thrashing.

"Mokoto! Do you want to get back on the boat now, or do you want to swim with Nui?" Lana shouted out.

Mokoto started to feel a familiar sense of fatigue wash over him after his celebratory antics with Nui. It had been a long, tiring, dramatic day. So he swerved his way over and the family pulled him back inside and laid him on the bench.

"You need to show us the way!" George reminded him.

"Nui will do that! Just follow her!" Mokoto knew they could rely on his trusted whale friend.

As Mokoto lay there, his eyes began to look heavy. George knew he needed to keep his scales moist if he was going to be out of the water for a few hours, so he grabbed a pile of towels that he kept for his whale watching customers, who often needed them after being soaked with sea spray, and reached over the side of the boat to drench them in the salty ocean. He carefully wrapped them around Mokoto's tail and left him to fall into a world of dreams.

As they all soaked in the enveloping sense of calm, the boat picked up speed again and trailed behind Nui as she faithfully led them towards the legendary tiny island next to The Coral Kingdom.

They had no idea, as they gently slipped out towards the horizon, that another boat was navigating its way back into the harbour, after a very long day at sea. The fishmonger was at the helm, feeling exceedingly pleased with himself, blissfully unaware that the next day, the marine biologists would track the transmitter to his shop and the police would arrest him for interfering with a government mission. His presence in the ocean at the time that the whale went missing didn't help his case.

# CHAPTER 20

The Pride of Kalani voyaged onwards under the guidance of its dependable navigator. It continued for five hours of smooth sailing, during which time Lana and Mia lay on the padded benches and drifted off into a peaceful slumber. A blanket of twinkling stars soothed them into dreamland, where images of happy whales danced in their heads.

It was still dark when a huge pod of dolphins started to carve their way through the water, alongside the boat. Nui's booming, pulsed calls to her playful friends woke Mokoto, who pulled his body up to look out over the side. There, Molailai leaped beside him, whistling a wondrous welcome and spinning out of the water with excitement at his best friend's arrival.

Lana was woken by Mokoto's soft laughter drifting through the breeze. She ambled over to Mokoto's side of the boat to look out over a carpet of blue-grey dolphins, stretching out as far as she could see, jumping through the waves and curving their dorsal fins in and out of the water at the same speed as the boat. She'd never seen anything like it.

"It's amazing!" she called out to George, at the wheel.

"Incredible!" George grinned back.

Lana knew Mia wouldn't want to miss this, so she tenderly nudged her. "Mia! Mia!" she whispered, "You have to see this!"

Mia rubbed her eyes and took a moment to figure out where she was. She smiled when she realised she was safely on the boat with Mokoto, and when she took in the endless expanse of dolphins beside them she gasped in awe.

They swept onwards, accompanied by their loyal army, when they passed through a colony of plankton. Stimulated by the motion, the plankton released a vast veil of luminescent, blue light, which made the ocean glow in the darkness like a swathe of sparkling sapphires. The dolphins dipped in and out of the glittering tapestry in mystical motion and Mia had to shake herself to make sure she wasn't still dreaming.

"It's called bioluminescence!" George's lack of sleep couldn't suppress his delight at this unworldly scene. "When the plankton detect motion, they release light to scare off predators," he explained, with a huge smile on his face.

"I'm going in!" Mokoto declared, unable to resist being part of the vibrant moving seascape that surrounded them.

He began to lift his body over the side, but struggled to hoist his tail up, so Lana and Mia helped him.

When Molailai saw Mokoto dive in, he soared over to him and leaped into the air, then plunged nose-first into the ocean where the two friends met under water and touched faces in an affectionate greeting. Their bodies soon burst out of the depths again and they flipped their tails in unison before gracefully shooting forward and spiralling through the water.

They were playing as they always had, but this time there was an extra dose of pleasure and energy in their well-fought freedom.

Molailai thrust his nose into the air and began to whistle, squeal and click. Right away, the other dolphins joined in with the same expressions, until the night air was filled with a glorious melody of dolphin sounds.

Mokoto swam up to Lana and Mia at the side of the boat, "It's all for you," he explained. "They're saying thank you, to both of you, and George! They want you to know how grateful they are!"

"Tell them it was the least we could do," Lana's smile radiated back at him, "for such beautiful, intelligent creatures!"

Mokoto relayed the message in Dolphish, through a series of clicks and whistles, before darting over to Nui, in front of the boat. For a moment, they both disappeared under water, but when they re-emerged, Mokoto was holding onto Nui's dorsal fin, and began to enjoy a thrilling ride on Nui's back as she lunged her enormous body in and out of the water.

"Can you see him?!" George called back to his sister and niece, making sure they didn't miss the breathtaking spectacle.

"Yes!" they sang out together, delighting at the scene.

The sun had just begun to peep out from the horizon, bringing a splendid blaze of orange and red that streaked through the darkness. Mokoto's body was silhouetted against this fiery palette as he continued to undulate forward, towards his enchanting home.

Mia was totally entranced. She scanned the magical scenery surrounding her and felt deeply privileged to be part of this unified force of beauty. The dolphins curved forward in their sea of luminescent, blue shimmering light, beneath a star-studded night sky that was just beginning to burst with layers of vibrant colour. Mokoto and Nui proudly ventured on at the forefront; majestic leaders of the captivating, moving picture.

Sunlight quickly began to coat the darkness, and very soon, the brilliant blue lights in the ocean faded away and the stars in the sky twinkled their goodbyes. As glorious, warm yellow hues sparkled on the water and reflected on the dolphins' smooth, sleek heads, a tiny island appeared in the distance. Lana and Mia gasped with excitement.

"That's it!" Mia cried out, "The island Grandpa told us about!"

Circled in turquoise and dotted with green, swaying palm trees, it glimmered in the distance with a beckoning charm.

"It's so perfect and small!" Lana exclaimed.

As they got closer, Nui and the dolphins dispersed into the surrounding water, so they didn't get beached near the shore. As Nui dived down, Mokoto let go of her fin and swam to the side of the boat, where Lana lifted the pearl from the middle of the lifebuoy and handed it to him. He then flexed his tail with a surge of power as he excitedly sped over to see his family and friends.

The Kalanis could see the merpeople dotted in the shallows, pointing at the boat and waving, so they waved back and watched with heart-melting happiness as they drew closer and clearly saw Mokoto's long, yellow hair and silver, blue and turquoise tail glide up into the lagoon. Two beautiful mermaids, one with long, orange hair and one with long, dark brown hair, slid over and lovingly wrapped their arms around him in a lingering embrace, before he showed them the pearl and began animatedly telling them about his adventures with the descendants of Kai Kalani.

George anchored the boat while Lana and Mia grabbed the boxes and they all waded through the clear water towards the beach. Shoals of yellow tang fish darted around their ankles and two resting manta rays waved their wings up from the sea bed as they fled from the disturbance.

"Hello!" George called out, as he ambled towards the collection of merpeople, waving enthusiastically and flashing a friendly smile.

"Come and meet my mum and sister!" Mokoto grinned, gesturing with his hand.

"He looks just how our ancestors described Kai Kalani!" Mokoto's mother whispered to her son with intrigue.

"Wow!" Noelani added, as she watched the legpeople approach them. "Look! It's like having four arms!"

The merpeople had intended to shower their guests with an overwhelming show of hospitality, but they underestimated how shocked they would feel seeing legpeople for the first time.

Mia gazed at the multitude of tails glimmering in the water as the merpeople sat up and stared at her in wonder. Each merperson seemed to have a set of three colours in their scales which made the shore line look as if it was draped in a vibrant, shimmering cloth. She was also struck by their exceptionally long hair that cascaded over their shoulders and down past their waists.

"We brought strawberries!" Lana announced, as she and Mia put the boxes down on the sand.

"Ooh!" came a chorus of gasps. Until now, strawberries had been the subject of legend.

Lana reached into one of the boxes and began handing out the sweet fruit, which was met with various groans and squeals of delight.

"Aren't they delicious?" Mokoto cried out, as he inhaled their delicate aroma.

"Exquisite!" Noelani agreed, with red juice seeping from her lips and dripping onto her orange hair.

The merpeople all wore garlands of red seaweed around their necks, and as the Kalanis took their places in the shallows, lying fully clothed amongst the merpeople, the mermaids closest to them removed their garlands and placed them over the heads of their guests.

Mokoto's mother then began to speak gently and eloquently, "Your ancestor, Kai Kalani, opened our minds to a whole world outside of The Coral Kingdom and left a fairy tale legacy of excitement and happiness. We honour him every year, in the Feast of Kai Kalani, where his spirit and energy are felt among us all. Now that you, his descendants, have appeared back into our lives to help us in our hour of need, we know that there is an enduring connection between us that can never be broken."

The other merpeople nodded in agreement while a hum of bubbly, gurgling sounds drifted over the group as they expressed their support in Mermish.

"You have saved my son, his best friend and his best friend's family, and safely returned them to us. For that, we shall be forever thankful, and we'd like to present you with a symbol of our gratitude."

She held up an enormous, soft pink conch shell from by her side and pressed her lips tightly together at the opening as she blew into it. The deep, powerful sound that it made reverberated around the group and brought a ceremonial feel to the meeting.

"This is for you," she passed the shell to Mia, who admired its immense size and delicate spirals before trying to blow it herself and letting out a weak squeak. The merpeople laughed affectionately.

"My great-grandmother was an adventurer who travelled a long way to find that shell," Mokoto's mother smiled warmly. "It's the biggest in our Kingdom. To us, it represents the joy of finding something unexpected and wonderful. And that's what we've found in you."

Noelani put her arm around Mia, who sank into her embrace.

"Thank you!" Mia muttered, feeling too overwhelmed to speak up.

"And George's father gave me this," Mokoto said, as he handed the giant pearl to his mother. "It's the pearl that was given by our merpeople to his great-great-grandfather, Kai Kalani, on one of his last visits to this island."

The merpeople leaned forward and gasped at how enormous the pearl was, gazing with admiration as the prized specimen shone brightly in the morning light.

"We want you to have it back," George added, "as a symbol of our friendship and a reminder that we'll always be here for you, whenever you need us."

"Thank you!" Mokoto's mother's soft, brown eyes, outlined by endlessly long, curled lashes, radiated warmth and appreciation. "I'll put it back on top of the arch at the entrance to the Coral Kingdom!"

While the merpeople marvelled at their returned pearl, George leaned over to his sister and whispered, "I think we have to go now Lanie, or I'll never make it back in time for my afternoon excursion."

"Okay," she replied, "but I definitely won't get to work on time!" Lana had never missed a day of work before, and ordinarily she'd be feeling anxious about taking time off, but right now she felt too relaxed and happy to care. "Come on," she nudged Mia, who was still resting her head against Noelani's shoulder. "It's time to leave."

The Kalanis took a while to give each of the merpeople a hug, before they came to Mokoto.

"Goodbye old friend," George pulled him in for a hug. "Thanks for the adventure. It's really been some-fin else!" he tried to mask his sinking, sweet sorrow with humour. "Some-FIN else, get it?!"

"Yes, I get it!" Mokoto shook his head hopelessly. He then paused and looked at his new friend with his doleful, blue eyes, "You risked everything for me and I'll never forget it. Thank you, George. You're an amazing legperson."

Lana was next to say farewell. She gave Mokoto a tight hug and closed her eyes to soak in the moment, before telling him, "I've loved getting to know you, but try not to come back again, okay?"

"Okay," Mokoto answered softly. "I'm sorry for all the trouble I've caused you. Thank you for everything."

"Mokoto," Lana replied, holding his forearms, "If I had to do it all again, I would. You're totally worth it."

Mia then crouched down in the crystal clear water at Mokoto's side and stared at his brown face. "This has been the best school holiday of my life," she told him. "I'm happy that you're back in the place where you belong, but I don't want it to end. You're my best friend, Mokoto. Our home's going to feel empty without you."

A single tear rolled down her flushed cheek as she glanced away to try and stem the pain.

"And my home feels complete with you," he answered, gently. "So you have to keep coming back to visit me! Your uncle has a boat, and you know where I am now."

"Can we?" Mia looked up at George, hopefully.

"Of course!" George agreed enthusiastically, feeling as grateful as Mia that this wasn't the last time they'd be seeing their mer-friend.

"Count the full moons," Mokoto told her. "On the sixth full moon from now, set off overnight, and I'll be waiting for you here in the morning! I can introduce you to the rest of the merpeople!"

"I can't wait!" Mia cried out, as she leaned forward and gave him a big hug.

"And please bring tea next time!" Mokoto asked, with a playful wink, as she pulled away from him.

"Definitely!" Mia agreed, before the family finally waded back towards The Pride of Kalani and climbed onboard.

Mokoto swam over and stayed next to the boat as it slowly moved away from the island, remaining with it as it drifted out of the turquoise tide and into the deeper blues. There, Molailai joined him and together they dived, leaped and spun alongside the vessel as Mia and Lana waved. In the distance, Mokoto's family and friends were waving goodbye too, watching Mia and her family disappear into the shimmering ocean.

As the boat picked up speed, Mokoto and Molailai knew it was time to slow down and head back to The Coral Kingdom for the delayed Feast of Kai Kalani, but before they turned around, Mokoto floated in the water and took a moment to watch Mia being sped away back to her land.

"Remember!" he called out to her in the warm ocean breeze, "This isn't the end, it's just the beginning!"

# EPILOGUE

Back on the land, the dolphinarium closed down permanently and a public swimming pool opened in its place.

George was so inspired by his dolphin encounter, he decided to take out a loan to buy another boat and branched out into dolphin watching expeditions. He hired Tomasi, the security guard at the old dolphinarium, to work for him and they struck up a great friendship. Whenever Tomasi saw Lana, however, he could never quite figure out who she reminded him of.

Lana couldn't get the surreal picture of dolphins swimming through vast swathes of luminescent plankton out of her head. She began to spend her spare time taking photographs of all the wondrous images the ocean had to offer and, before long, it turned into full-time work. She left her office job to become a marine photographer and was wildly successful.

Grandpa Frank had a new-found fascination with seagulls and spent a large part of each day sitting at the open living room window, observing the birds through his binoculars and trying to communicate with them in the same way that Mokoto did. A few had learned to answer his calls and he rewarded them with handfuls of bird seed that they pecked from his palm. He was too infirm to travel long distances again, but the memories he treasured of Mokoto were enough to last a lifetime.

Mia kept a picture of Mokoto, which she'd cut out of the newspaper, stuck to her dressing table mirror. She returned to her usual life of school and surfing with an extra spring in her step, knowing that she was stronger and more capable than anyone around her could possibly imagine. Whenever life's mundanities threatened to get her down, she reminded herself of how lucky and special she was, because she had magical insight into a whole other, enchanted existence that no one else outside her family knew about. At night, she'd often look up at the stars from her bedroom window and wonder if Mokoto was enjoying the same view from the surface of his watery Kingdom.

The gigantic conch shell from The Coral Kingdom took centre stage on the dining table in the Kalani's apartment, serving as a beautiful, enduring reminder of the family's close connection to the merpeople.

Every six months, under the light of a full moon, George, Lana and Mia would venture out to their secret island and meet up with Mokoto and his family. Each time, they were introduced to more members of the The Coral Kingdom community and lavished them with big boxes of fresh strawberries and flasks full of tea. The two groups shared laughter and friendship, but they all knew, in their hearts, that this idyllic white sand beach was the only place where their worlds should ever overlap.

Nui migrated to cooler waters, safe in the knowledge that her friends would all be there when she returned. Mokoto continued to get distracted by Molailai's playfulness when he was sent out to gather seaweed, Noelani spent lots of time lost in daydreams and perfecting her braiding skills, and life in The Coral Kingdom continued, in all its glorious simplicity.

**THE END**

SARAH TAVOLA